MacKenzie Saves the World

Jamie DeBree

Brazen Snake Books
Billings Montana

MacKenzie Saves the World

Copyright 2014 by Jamie DeBree
First paperback edition 2023
Published by Brazen Snake Books
Cover Art Credits
© Coliap | Dreamstime.com (World)
© Libux77 | Dreamstime.com (Superhero)

This book is a work of fiction and any resemblance to persons, living or dead, or places, events or locales is purely coincidental. The characters are productions of the author's imagination, and used fictitiously.

For comic book and food lovers everywhere.

Chapter 1

Propping the large box between her hip and the concrete wall, MacKenzie Jones jiggled her keys with her right hand trying to find the one the mall manager had given her just a week before. The box shifted and she caught it with her left arm and a quick hip-twist, wrenching her shoulder in the process. At the clang of her keys hitting the ground, she grunted and stomped her foot in frustration, nearly dropping the box again.

Damn it. Where was a superhero when you needed one, anyways?

The thought of putting the heavy box down and having to pick it up again was daunting, to say the least. It had been doable to get it from the back of her car, but off the ground? That might hurt. And her muscles were already sore from painting, putting displays together and stocking the shelves to get ready for the grand opening three days from now.

Kenzie's Comics. She was going to dedicate opening day to all those kids at school who constantly put her down either for reading all the time, or reading the wrong things. She'd never been in sync with anyone back then it seemed, and despite everyone either ignoring or ridiculing her, she'd gone on to graduate near the top of her class.

In college she'd decided to study both business and fine arts, which hadn't made her popular with either of those peer groups, and she'd constantly felt pulled to choose one or the other. Ignoring the pressure, she'd graduated with a major in business and a minor in art, and now here she was, the proud owner of the comic book shop she'd dreamed of opening since she was sixteen years old.

Her parents were skeptical, but only because the market for comics seemed slim to non-existent these days. But Kenzie was convinced it was there, if she could just get the word out that she was open for business. The prime space she'd leased in the Brookfield Mall was the first step to doing just that, she hoped.

If she could get into the back door, and by extension her new store, that is.

Looking down at her keys again, she shifted to sandwich the box more firmly between her body and the wall, and then bent forward as much as she dared, her arm a good six inches too short.

"Need some help?"

She straightened as much as possible and turned her head to see a very expensive-looking navy blue tie with a purple paisley pattern staring back at her. Craning her neck, she looked up, up, up past a perfectly tapered chest and broad, powerful-looking shoulders until she finally met the amused gaze of a man who was entirely too Clark Kent-without-glasses for his own good.

Or hers, for that matter.

Ever since she'd grown out of her awkward high school ugly-duckling phase, men had actually seemed drawn to her appearance. It was an affliction that lasted exactly as long as it took them to decide that she was either too smart or too artsy for their personal taste, and then they moved on without a backward glance. With this guy, it was definitely the artist he'd object to, so she did her best to look smart. Whatever smart looked like.

"Actually, if you could just hand me my keys - they're over there. I dropped them."

She mentally rolled her eyes even as the words left her mouth. Of course she'd dropped them. Repeating the obvious. Smart. Very smart.

Kent stooped to pick up her keys, and Kenzie figured that as long as no one ever found out, it was okay that she watched the collar of his shirt to see if a flash of blue peeked out as it pulled just slightly with the effort. Superheroes didn't actually exist of course, but plenty of girls fantasized that they did. Or so she kept telling herself.

Only somewhat disappointed when the only blue she saw was his tie, she took the keys from him with a smile, enjoying the little dimple in his cheek as he returned the gesture and reached for the box.

"Here. Let me carry that in for you. I'm headed that way too."

There was a brief moment of awkward fumbling when he slid his hands in close to relieve her of her burden before she could object, brushing a couple parts of her body that hadn't seen any action in years and sending an embarrassing warmth up into her cheeks. When he finally stepped back, box in hand, she looked down at her keys, quickly found the right one and unlocked the door, proud of herself for managing the task with shaking hands.

"So you...ah...own a store here too?" she asked, pulling the door open with relief and forcing herself to look up at him again. Gadzooks, the man was tall. And still looking amused, which wasn't helping at all.

He stepped inside, stopping to wait for her before he nodded at another plain metal door on the left with a stenciled sign that read "Taste the World".

"The storefront for my catering business. We do some minimal prep work and small orders here, and I own a professional kitchen in a warehouse a few blocks away where we fill the larger orders. Which one's yours?" He glanced down the dim corridor at the other shop entries, and then back at her, eyebrows raised.

"That's where all the good smells come from," she said with a smile. "I swear I gain weight some days just smelling all that food from your store." She pointed to the door just to the left of his. "That's mine," she said, finding the right key and leading the way. "Kenzie's Comics. We're opening at the end of the week." Unlocking the door, she held it open and waited for him to go inside.

"You can just put that on that long table," she said, flicking on the lights to illuminate her office-slash-stockroom. "Are you reader?"

"Of comic books?" He chuckled. "No, I'm afraid not, though I've been known to pick up a novel occasionally when I have time. Aren't these mostly written for kids and high school students who like those role playing games?"

She stifled a sigh, and reminded herself that part of the reason for opening a comic book store was to educate people about comic books, and be an ambassador for the format. Pasting a smile on her face, she did her best not to sound condescending as she answered.

"A lot of people enjoy comic books, and there are a lot of

different types of stories in this format to choose from. Have you ever tried them?" She turned to one of the shelves on the wall where stacks of comics were neatly organized. "You're a foodie - I know I have a food-themed series here somewhere, but it might be out on the shelf already. It's called The Restaurateur, and--"

"That's okay. Don't go to any trouble," he said, and when she turned to look at him, he was backing toward the door. "I actually have to go. I'm already late and Andrea's waiting, but maybe after you're open, I'll come in and check it out. I'll talk to you later - gotta run."

And just like that, he was gone, the door shutting behind him with a very final heavy click. She stared at it, marveling at how quickly he'd disappeared - and all because she'd offered him a comic book.

She didn't even know his name.

Obviously not someone who would be interested in trading goods or cross-promoting. Which was kind of a shame, since they were mall neighbors and all.

Getting the box cutter off of her desk, she carefully opened the box he'd carried in for her, and started taking the latest shipment of books out and sorting them into piles. Some would stay on the stock shelves for later, others would go out front to the new displays. Trevor Markum, the one employee they'd hired could take care of that later, but there was a specific issue in this box that she wanted to look at before anyone else. And near the bottom, she found it.

The cover of Charade winked up at her beneath the florescent work lights, and she lifted out the stack, counting out the ten copies she'd ordered before putting all but two on the table next to the others. She placed one on Kevin Peters' desk - her only long-term friend and business partner. He'd pitched in a third of the start-up costs for the shop, and planned to help out with sales and subscriptions a few days a week, but his main focus was on his writing. Kenzie was perfectly happy with that, and knew he'd be in today to help out with a few things.

She took the final copy of Charade with her to her desk, settling in her chair to examine the lines, the shadows, the colors, the nuances that had taken hours to make exactly right.

It was perfect. More importantly, it was her first real contract as an artist, and she still couldn't believe that she and Kevin had created something so wonderful together. Slowly turning the pages, she read the story he'd written for the millionth time, noting how the words and her illustrations worked together to introduce readers to Charade, the female superhero they'd created over many long nights and several years worth of planning and practice.

It was all up to the readers now. If they embraced Charade, MacKenzie and Kevin would hopefully enjoy a long run writing and illustrating the series, with more work to come. If not, well, it was back to the drawing board.

Unable to stop smiling, she took her copy out to the front of the store where an empty frame hung just behind sales counter. Carefully placing the copy inside, she hung it back up and made sure it was straight, standing back to admire the view for just a couple more seconds.

The back door clicked shut again, and she went back to the office, eager to see Kevin's face when he picked up their first comic book.

* * * * *

Josh Taylor felt like a total jerk, running off on his cute, geeky new neighbor. But in his experience, girls like that tended to latch on at any sign of interest at all, and he didn't need that type of complication right now. And cute as they were, geeky girls like that were...different. He didn't mind personally, of course, but there were his friends to consider, and his family. Someone like her just wouldn't fit in his world. It was too much to ask, or it had been the few times he'd tried.

He let himself into the back of the catering shop, taking in a deep whiff of the sweet caramel and cinnamon scent wafting through the air. Andrea, his sister, would just be finishing up the morning baking and getting ready for whatever orders they needed to fill this afternoon. She ran the kitchen, her culinary degrees put to good use in the business they'd started five years earlier. Loving to eat, but never quite mastering the art of boiling water, Josh kept the business side running smoothly with his love of organization and head for numbers. He also tended to have a better tableside manner than his more passionate sister.

"Josh? Is that you?" Andrea's voice came from his office, and he followed it to find his sister in his chair, frantically rifling through the papers on his desk.

"Sorry I'm late," he said, relieved when she looked up, her hands still for the moment. "What are you looking for?"

"The number for the Fairchild's event planner. That weird recipe they gave me for the canapes doesn't work - it won't set up, and I can substitute, but not without their okay and the party is tonight so we need to get this figured out like three hours ago and why isn't that file right on top since the party's tonight?"

He held up both hands, approaching slowly. "I'll call and get approval - Pete Fairchild is still infatuated with you, so I'm sure whatever you want to do will be fine. And the file is right on top - of my inbox. That blue folder with the Fairchild label right on top. See it?" He almost managed to keep a straight face, but his lips twitched up just a tad, and from the dark look on his sister's face, she hadn't missed it.

"Well you don't have to be smug about it. And where were you anyways? There's a last minute catering order that needs to go to the warehouse as soon as possible, and we had a walk-in who wants twenty-four cookies for a party this afternoon at three."

He frowned. "We don't do cookie orders."

She nodded her head, eyes wide with panic. "I know that, you know that, but apparently Jenna doesn't know that yet, and she took the payment and put the order on our calendar. I figured it would be bad business to cancel it."

He sighed and sat down in his chair as she moved out from behind his desk. Andrea had hired Jenna herself, not bothering to consult him first. The girl was young - barely out of a two year finishing school and not exceptionally bright, but was the daughter of one of their father's lawyer friends, which had been Andrea's justification for skipping the interview process. He suspected his sister was hoping he and Jenna would hit it off - something he had absolutely no interest in.

"I'll talk to Jenna, and I'll send the cookie order to the warehouse shop on a special rush. As for where I was - Mom called this morning and caught me before I got out the door. She said she needed to check our availability for a friend's party next month, but I think she really just wanted to know if you're still seeing that kitchen rep from last month, since apparently you won't answer your phone…" he raised an eyebrow.

Andrea just shrugged. "I don't want to talk about it. And for future reference, he's old news. But Mat said he saw you pull up twenty minutes ago, and then he saw you talking to some girl. Anything you wanna tell me, little brother?"

He rolled his eyes. "I helped the woman from that new shop next door carry a box in. Sue me for being gentlemanly."

Andrea wrinkled her nose. "You mean the comic shop? I still don't understand why they had to locate her right next to us. Why can't she be on the other end of the mall next to the toy shop and that other bookstore? And why would any girl in her right mind want to run a comic store anyways? I mean, obviously she's not worried about attracting a real man, right?" She looked pointedly at Josh, who merely shrugged. Andrea was just as bad as the rest of his family when it came to classism and looking down on anyone who didn't measure up to the sort of ideals and income level they personally had. Sometimes she tried to hide it, but apparently the claws were out today.

It made him sick, honestly. He often wondered if he'd been adopted.

"Don't you have canapes or something to make? I thought you were in a hurry?"

She gave him a strange, knowing look. "Don't go there again, Josh. For all of our sakes. You know what the last geek-girl you brought home did to our family…not to mention to you personally. It's not good for anyone, brother-dear. Find yourself a nice doctor or lawyer - or better yet, the daughter of one who wants to stay home and take care of you. You know that's the only way to make the family happy."

With that, she turned and walked away. It never ceased to

amaze him how little everyone around him thought of actually being happy, rather than making everyone think they were happy.

He made a few calls and got everything back on an even keel, and then went out to the floor to go over the list of services with the new hostess for the third time in a week.

For the twenty minutes he spoke with her, he got the feeling Jenna wasn't listening to a word he said. Judging from the dreamy look in her eyes, she was more focused on getting his personal attention than actually learning how to do her job. Which, ironically, would have been more attractive.

Finally giving up and leaving her with a copy of the list he hoped she'd actually study, he went back to his office, made sure everything was going smoothly with the Fairchild account, and decided to see if Andrea wanted to get lunch.

She wasn't in the kitchen, and when he went to the front of the store, Jenna just pointed to the mall entrance where he could hear Andrea's agitated voice carrying far and wide.

Just what they needed. The mall owners already disliked her for her rather opinionated stance on...well, everything, and this was not going to help. It wasn't like her to berate the customers though, and he hurried to see who it was on the other end of her apparently long-winded rant.

Pushing through the door into the mall, he mentally winced at the sight of his sister yelling something about offensive window displays at the comic book girl next door, who was standing there with her arms crossed, nibbling her bottom lip with an outward display of calm that would have been convincing aside from the redness creeping up her neck and into her cheeks, and the flare of anger in her eyes.

He also noticed the two security guards headed their way, flanked by a short guy in an ill-fitting suit that had to be the mall manager.

"Andrea," he said, moving between her and the comic shop girl. "You're making a scene, and the manager is on his way. You know we can't afford another strike with the owners. Calm down."

She shrugged off the hand on her shoulder, her eyes never leaving the other woman, who had moved back a few steps to give him room.

"I know he's on the way. I called him. Look at those posters she has hanging in her windows! Those women have no clothes! It's obscene, and it's going to scare our customers away!"

Josh examined the display in question. Andrea was right that the women on the posters were rather scantily clad, but all the pertinent bits were covered, and while he didn't know much about comic books or characters, he seemed to remember the cartoon versions being similarly dressed when he was a kid.

"I think this might be something to discuss in the office rather than out here, don't you?" he said, keeping his voice low and even. "I'm sure we can reach some sort of--"

Andrea glared at him, her green eyes blazing. "I should have known you'd take her side. Of course you would. Just because you have a thing for geeky, intelligent girls, you'd go against your own sister. Your own business, for that matter." She looked past him, and her eyes narrowed.

"I'm sure Mr. Williams will agree with me that this display is inappropriate for the type of clientele we want to bring in here, don't you?"

They all turned to look at the manager as he stepped closer to the window. Josh wasn't sure what he could possibly see as close as he was, but considering the slight quirk of the man's lips, he suspected Andrea wasn't going to win this round.

"Are you familiar with comic books at all, Ms. Taylor?" the manager asked.

Andrea shook her head, her expression one of extreme distaste.

"Of course not. I'd never read something so...base. Especially not as an adult."

Mr. Williams nodded, and then turned to the comic shop owner. Josh was truly surprised she'd remained quiet all this time. Most of the women he knew would have been yelling right back, adding to the cacophony.

"Ms. Jones, do you think that perhaps you could feature more action-themed covers on this side of the store, and these more...dramatic covers on the other side of your doorway, away from Ms. Taylor's storefront?"

Andrea opened her mouth to argue, but Josh clamped a firm hand down on her shoulder, giving her a hard stare. It seemed like a perfectly reasonable compromise to him, though Ms. Jones would be well within her contract to insist on keeping the display as is.

"I can do that," the woman answered, nodding slowly as she surveyed the front of her shop. "Maybe I can work something out with the clothing store as far as cross-promotion goes. They have some great evening dresses in there."

Mr. Williams smiled, and patted her arm - a condescending gesture Josh was fairly certain the woman didn't appreciate, but tolerated all the same. The manager turned to Andrea next, eyebrows raised.

"Is that acceptable to you, Ms. Taylor?"

Josh didn't give her a chance. "That will be fine, Mr. Williams." He shook the man's hand, and then turned to Ms. Jones. "Thank you, for accommodating us. We really appreciate it."

She gave him a curt nod, one side of her mouth turned up in a wry smile.

"You're welcome. Even us geeky, intelligent girls can be reasoned with when asked nicely."

With that, she turned and went back into her store, the lock snapping shut with a loud click behind her. Seconds later, she was standing in the window display, starting to move the posters and books she'd put up.

"I do expect that things will be...peaceful between your two stores," Mr. Williams said. "Ms. Jones has been a pleasure to work with throughout the process of getting her set up here at Brookfield Mall, and her store may well bring in a lot of repeat business for all of us. We would hate to lose her as a tenant."

He turned and walked away, the security guards trailing behind him. Andrea huffed beside Josh.

"What the hell did he mean by that?" she asked as he led her back into their store.

Josh looked at her and shook his head. "It means that if you and Ms. Jones can't get along, she's not the one they'll get rid of. So stay away from her, Sis. Business real estate is expensive these days, and we're running on a tight margin as is."

"So I'm just supposed to watch her chase all of our business away and be happy about it? How's that going to help our margins?"

"Or you could just keep an open mind, and think of ways we

can market to her clientele, get them in our doors after they come out of hers." He let that sink in a minute, watching her process it. She didn't buy the idea yet, but at least he'd planted the seed.

"I'm going to get lunch - you want anything?"

She shook her head. "I'm going to the warehouse to pack up the party tonight. I won't be back today. Are you coming tonight?"

He nodded. "I'll stop in for a few minutes, just to make an appearance. See you then?"

She shrugged, clearly still upset as she went back to the kitchen. Going out the front door again, he waved at Ms. Jones in her window as he walked toward the food court, receiving only a slight nod in return.

Women.

Chapter 2

Kenzie nodded at Mr. Taylor when he waved, refraining from the instinct to give him the finger instead. It was his sister she was really mad at - that bitch could just go to hell for all she cared, but if he really did have a thing for geeky intellectuals like his sister said, that meant he had something against her personally to have run out so quickly that morning.

And that hurt, dammit.

She finished the window displays, working through lunch to get it all done, and stepping back behind a life-sized cardboard cutout of superwoman when she saw Taylor walking back to his store. He glanced at the windows, and then stopped for a closer look, and she considered jumping out to scare him at one point. He didn't seem to have much of a sense of humor though, and all she needed was two complaints to the manager in one day. Not a great impression when her store wasn't even open yet.

After he'd gone, she finished up, said a hasty goodbye to Trevor still working in the stock room, and rushed home for a quick dinner. Mandy Fairchild, an old friend from college had invited...well, begged her, really...to go to a party her parents were throwing tonight. Born into wealth by mistake, she often said, Mandy enjoyed her family's social status but was often bored at the big parties, and more often stuck trying to entertain a bevy of eligible bachelors her mother sent her way.

Kenzie had reconnected with her at a comic convention, of all places, where Mandy had been just blowing off steam with friends. They'd found they had a lot in common, and Mandy had taken it upon herself to find Kenzie that special someone - a task Kenzie thought was dubious at best. But when presented with the opportunity to attend the function tonight, Kenzie had readily agreed. She was always looking to enhance her social connections. Her business was counting on it now.

At precisely seven that night, she was dressed to the nines in her trusty little black sheath and ready to go.

At seven-twenty, she quit pacing, and reminded herself that Mandy was always late. Always. Taking up vigil by the window, she slid her shoes off to give her feet a quick reprieve from the three-inch heels.

At seven-forty, a car finally pulled up out front, and she slid her feet into her shoes, grabbed the small clutch with her keys, cell phone and business cards inside, and hurried out to the curb where a driver was holding the back door open.

"Ms. MacKenzie Jones?" he asked. She nodded, frowning as she bent down and saw a man's legs and shoes on the other side of the seat. "Is Mandy…"

The man leaned across the seat, and she scowled at the familiar face of her new mall neighbor as he grinned up at her, patting the seat beside him.

"Mandy was running incredibly late, as usual. She called and begged me to pick up her friend on the way to the party. If that's okay with you, of course."

"Um…sure. I guess," she said, sliding into the car just far enough that the driver could close the door, but staying well away from Taylor. "If you can stand to be near me that long, of course. It seemed like you couldn't get away from me fast enough this morning. Though now that I've met your...sister, is it? I guess that explains a lot."

She could feel him staring at the side of her face, but she kept her eyes trained out the front window.

"My sister doesn't speak for me," he said, his tone firm, but even. "And I'm sorry she treated you like that. It was...inexcusable, and it won't happen again."

Kenzie gave a small laugh, and shook her head, looking down at the clutch in her lap. "You're not your sister's keeper, Mr. Taylor. And I think we both know that she'll eventually find something else to rant at me about. I get the feeling it's not just comics she has it in for, but me, in particular."

"Call me Josh, please," he said, leaning forward until she had no choice but to look at him. A mistake, as she knew it would be, because that handsome face of his should require some sort of license to carry. "May I call you Kenzie?"

She shrugged. "Normally only friends call me that, but I suppose since it's on my sign..."

"Well hopefully you'll consider me a friend eventually. And yes, my sister has issues with comic books and what she calls 'low-brow' entertainment in general. As for girls like you...that's my fault, I'm afraid. The women in my family are brought up to be smart, but to stay in their place. If they step outside the boundaries at all, they're dealt with swiftly and harshly. The last time I brought a woman home who refused to respect what the family expected from women, they ate her alive - out of jealousy, I presume."

Kenzie shook her head. "That doesn't make any sense. They

choose to put up with those constraints. It's just...wrong, on so many levels."

He bobbed his head noncommittally. "Technically, yes, it's a choice. But presumably, you were raised in an environment where you were encouraged to make that choice. The women in my family - our social circle, really - are raised with the knowledge that if they step too far out of line, they'll be ostracized from all their family and friends, and cut off from the life they know. If you think about it, it's not an easy thing to just give all that up when you can find ways to play along and still remain in the life you've always known. And everyone does it, to some extent. I'll bet even you respect some social or familial boundaries just to stay in your family's good graces, don't you?"

MacKenzie considered that as the car rolled to a stop outside the luxurious Fairchild mansion. The driver opened Josh's door first, which annoyed her more than it should due to their current conversation. As she turned to get out, Josh was there, holding out a hand to help, and she took it, feeling a jolt of awareness at the touch of skin on skin.

Of course that's why he got out first, she realized. To help the poor, helpless female who had to be kept in her place. The thought stuck with her like a grain of sand rubbing the wrong way as he crooked his arm and she took it naturally, as if she couldn't walk herself up to the door.

"I can feel you thinking," he whispered, grinning when she frowned up at him. "And maybe you are playing right into the same old outdated patriarchal moves that smart girls such as yourself should know to avoid. Or maybe..." he stopped, pulling her to the side of the door as another couple walked past and through the door, both giving them an inquisitive look as they went past.

"Maybe I just wanted you close," he said, his penetrating stare making her weak in the knees. "Maybe I was using those social niceties to touch something forbidden, even if just for a few minutes."

MacKenzie was speechless. She stared, trying to decide how to react if he wanted to strip off that mild-mannered-businessman persona and fly her off to his ice-caves or something. Would it make her a horrible sell-out to her gender if she did?

Did she even care?

A loud, irritating squeal sadly characteristic of said gender broke the spell, and they both turned to see Mandy flying toward them at top-speed. How she did that on four-inch heels was anyone's guess, but MacKenzie braced for impact as her friend ran up and pulled her into a hug.

"You're finally here! Say thank you to Josh so we can go - I have about a zillion men I want you to meet so we can make fun of them later, and the caterer made some canapés that are to die for, and Mom is having a fit that they aren't the recipe she wanted. Thank God for that, since her recipe sucks." Mandy wiggled her fingers and grinned at Josh, grabbed MacKenzie's hand and pulled her through the door before MacKenzie could say anything at all.

* * * * *

Josh wiggled his fingers back at Mandy, trying to decide if he was glad she'd broken his moment with Kenzie, or annoyed. Not that it mattered much. He wouldn't put another girl through what Morgan had to endure at the hands of his family. So it was probably just as well that things had ended where they did.

19

Hopefully Kenzie wasn't the type to read more into the situation than there actually was.

Except if she thought he was interested, she'd be right.

He tried to stay away from her for the first part of the evening, but found it nearly impossible. Whenever he entered a room and she was there, his eyes were drawn to her. Whenever he left a room, it seemed like she and Mandy entered whatever space he'd gone to shortly thereafter.

Finally, around nine o'clock, he settled into a comfortable couch in the main hall and watched the women as they danced, talked, flirted, and just generally enjoyed the party. As the night wore on, he watched the expression on Kenzie's face go from open and excited to closed, tired, and more withdrawn. It crossed his mind to offer her a ride home, and he had nearly convinced himself to go to her when Andrea sat down beside him.

"I thought you were only going to make an appearance, brother-dear. What has you staying so late?"

He shrugged and gave her a smile. "Nothing in particular. I've just been watching people, for the most part. How goes the job? Mandy was raving about your canapés earlier..."

She wrinkled her nose. "Ms. Fairchild - the elder, I mean - has been whining about them all night to everyone who'll listen. Luckily I don't think it's hurting our reputation any. I personally saw a few people sympathizing with her, and then grabbing another one off a tray not five minutes later."

She scanned the crowd, her eyes narrowing and her smile fading at something a few feet to their right. Josh didn't need to look to know what she was scowling at. Or rather, who.

"What is she doing here?" Andrea looked at him, and then

back at the offending party. Her eyes widened. "That's why you're still here. Because of her? Josh…"

He looked over to see MacKenzie and Mandy standing with Ms. Fairchild, one of the waiters holding a tray of hor d'oeurves for the women to choose from. Ms. Fairchild sighed as she and Mandy picked a salmon baguette, while MacKenzie chose one of the now-infamous canapés.

"Those are horrible, dear…here, put it back and choose something else. I can't imagine what the catering company was thinking, substituting this terrible recipe for my great grandmother's. They come highly recommended, of course, and the owners are dear friends of my husbands, but I really don't see how we can use Taste the World again after this…debacle."

Mackenzie merely popped the canapé into her mouth and chewed carefully, her expression thoughtful. After she'd finished, she smiled.

"I'll have to disagree with you on that, I'm afraid. Those are wonderful…can-a-pays, did you call them? Whatever they're called, they're delicious, though I'm sure your family recipe is wonderful too. All the food has been fabulous tonight, Ms. Fairchild. I think your catering company did a wonderful job."

Josh grinned wide. "There. Of all the people in this place, the one you can't stand stood up for your food - our company. Aren't you glad she's here now?"

Surprising him, Andrea shot him a look of shock and dismayed disbelief.

"You can't honestly be serious," she said, shaking her head. "Watch."

Ms. Fairchild was laughing, though the uneasy look on Mandy's face implied that wasn't a good thing.

"Oh, I remember you. You're the friend from college - the poor one. What is it you're doing now, dear? Opening some kind of store in the mall?"

MacKenzie nodded, her smile gone, but her chin up. "That's right. I own a comic book store. We open in two days."

Ms. Fairchild flipped a hand down in a dismissive gesture. "Well that explains it, then. You can't be expected to have a refined palate, can you? It would stand to reason that someone like you would have more...simplistic tastes, dear. I'm glad you like them." She turned to Mandy, who wasn't bothering to hide her anger now. "Don't you girls stay up too late now. You know what late nights do to your eyes, darling."

The woman walked off, and Mandy turned to MacKenzie, but Josh couldn't make out what they were saying. Andrea shrugged.

"See? Her opinion doesn't matter here. If anything, it reinforced Fairchild's conviction, because if someone beneath her likes them, they must be bad." She stood, her expression part sympathy, and part resignation.

"I said it before, and I'll say it again. Stay away, Josh. Your world is too different - it can't work."

He watched MacKenzie walk away, Mandy running after her, and got to his feet. It was all so stupid. So unnecessary.

"Yeah. Well maybe it's time to switch worlds," he murmured, brushing past his sister. He moved quickly to the front door and out onto the sprawling concrete porch just in time to see the women get into Mandy's car and peel out of the driveway. He wanted to follow them, to talk to Kenzie and make sure she was okay. He hesitated a long moment before walking to his car.

His driver silently opened the door and Josh slid into the back seat. There was the business to think about, and the fact that his parents owned a third of it. It was ridiculous, the rampant elitism that he generally pretended to ignore, but it was real, and something he couldn't just brush aside for the sake of a girl he didn't really even know.

And tonight, at least, she had Mandy.

"Where to, Sir?" the driver asked.

Josh rubbed his forehead with one hand and overruled his instincts. "Home, please."

Chapter 3

The next morning, MacKenzie parked in the staff lot behind the mall and found the right key to the building before she got out. She hurried into her store, relieved when she didn't run into either Josh or his sister. The grand opening was just one day away, and the last thing she needed was the distraction of those two when she was trying to take care of last-minute details.

Not that she could actually get Josh out of her head. It seemed that after their conversation last night, and then that incredibly hot, intimidating moment outside the mansion, he'd taken up residence at the forefront of her mind and refused to leave.

Damn the man. He was strictly off-limits, regardless of his apparent interest in her. It was probably just rebelliousness on his part, she figured. Poor little rich guy trying to break free from the chains of aristocracy, and using whatever female free spirit he could find to help him do it.

Wrinkling her nose, she looked around and shook her head, realizing she'd made it all the way to her desk without being aware of her surroundings.

"Get out of my head!" she murmured, logging into her computer and pulling up the checklist for her final day before opening. It was long, but doable, and she smiled, her skin all tingly with the knowledge that at ten tomorrow morning, her dream would finally come true. Free snacks, coffee and comic books (one each, with purchase) for everyone! It was going to be great.

She spent the next hour going through emails, updating the social media pages for the store and checking off list items. Trevor came in and started setting up the table out front and Kevin appeared half-an-hour later to work on their latest Charade book.

When the phone rang and her friend Sheila's number showed up on the caller ID, she grinned. Sheila had offered to bake a bunch of cookies, brownies and other bite-sized treats to serve, and Kenzie had gladly taken her up on it.

"Sheila - hi! How's the baking going? Need anything?"

The snuffling in her ear wiped the smile from her face.

"Kenzie, I'm so sorry..." Sheila sniffed again, and Kenzie couldn't decide if the cause was a cold or emotional distress. "It's Lily. Kenz, I had to put her down today. She fell and you know how weak she was anyways, and the vet didn't think she'd survive surgery at her age..." Sheila's voice broke, and Kenzie's heart broke listening to the obvious pain.

"I'm so, so sorry, Sheila. What can I do? Want me to come over?"

Another sniffle. "You don't have to do that - I know you're busy getting ready for the opening, and Damon's here with me. But Kenz, I can't get those treats done for tomorrow. I just can't. I'm so sorry."

Kenzie shook her head. "Of course you can't hon. Don't you worry about a thing - I'll take care of it. I appreciate you letting me know, and I'm so sorry about your dog."

"Thanks Kenzie. Call me tomorrow, K? I know it's going to be great, but I want details." *Sniffle.*

"I will - I promise. I'll talk to you tomorrow."

Kenzie hung up the phone and sighed. Something had been bound to happen - things were going too well. And now she'd have to dip into her already depleted budget and find something to serve tomorrow with just the afternoon to get something lined up.

And just next door, there was a caterer who might have some samples left over she could buy at a discounted price. If she didn't talk to Andrea, anyways. It was likely she'd run into Josh though, a scary thought, but it really was the most efficient option. She didn't have time to run all over town and still finish her list.

The decision made, she got her business debit card, checked the spreadsheets and told Trevor she'd be back soon. Steeling herself for the worst, she took a deep breath and let herself out the front doors of the shop.

Taste the World was an elegant storefront, and MacKenzie felt both under-dressed and out of her element as she walked into the pristine cream and brown showroom. It was set up more like a jewelry store than a food joint, with thick, high-pile chocolate carpet on the floor, soothing cream-colored walls and an elegant, lace-stenciled brown border near the ceiling.

Several round tables were strategically placed throughout the room and covered with thick cream cloths, with square tiers and trays of miniature foods artfully arranged on each one. Fancy little tents of heavy card stock sat near each different item, revealing the names in beautiful calligraphy, and inviting guests to please take one.

It was a far cry from the explosion of color and movement in her own store, and Kenzie was careful not to touch anything as she made her way through the tables to the long, white-marble counter on its chocolate wood pedestal at the back of the store.

The girl behind it - she couldn't have been more than twenty - looked up with a smile. Her eyes took in the comfortable jeans and black Charade t-shirt MacKenzie had worn that day, and her smile slowly faded to a cool, eyebrows raised stare.

"Can I help you?" she asked, her tone saying just the opposite. MacKenzie abandoned all hope of not seeing Josh at that moment, knowing he was the only one who could help her, if he would. Hitching her shoulders back and her chin up, she nodded.

"I need to see Mr. Taylor, please. Tell him it's Ms. Jones."

The girl looked a little shocked when MacKenzie matched her haughty tone. She didn't argue though, and picked up the phone, murmuring something quietly into the receiver. When she hung up, her expression was all business.

"He'll be right out. He's in a meeting that's just finishing up."

"Thank you." MacKenzie turned and wandered slowly around the tables, looking at the samples and mentally assessing what might work for her opening, and what might be a turn-off for her cheese puffs-and-soda crowd. When Josh finally came through the door behind the counter, she'd made a mental list of her five best choices, intending to ask for two and hope she could afford the price.

Her hopes dimmed when Andrea and Mr. Williams, the mall manager followed him out. All three looked frustrated and tired, which did not bode well for her request.

"Everything okay?" she asked, as the three of them

approached. Josh shook his head, but Andrea answered.

"Apparently some shoppers complained about the run-in between us the other day. It was our third strike. Mr. Williams here was just serving us our eviction notice. So it looks like you win, and we're out. Happy?"

Kenzie frowned, shaking her head. She didn't like Andrea, but it seemed like a thin reason to kick them out of the mall. Besides, she could really use their services, today, at least.

"No, of course not. Mr. Williams, there's nothing you can do?"

He gave her a strange look. "I'd have thought you'd be happy about this, Ms. Jones. Ms. Taylor isn't exactly a fan of your shop. It'll be easier for you with someone more...suitable next door."

"Actually," Kenzie looked at the sample tables. "I came over here today because I have a problem, and this would be the easiest way to solve it. I was kind of hoping we could work together, at least temporarily. If it goes well, we could both expand our customer bases, and bring in more business..."

"What did you have in mind?" Josh asked.

MacKenzie took a breath. She'd all but scrapped the cross-promotional ideas when Andrea had so vehemently attacked her, but maybe if she could sell them on it now, it would save their store and help hers in the process. At this point, there was nothing to lose by asking, and it might be the only time the Taylors needed her help.

"I actually have a long-term proposal in my office, but my immediate problem is that a friend who was supposed to bring the snacks for our grand opening tomorrow won't be able to follow through after all. So for today, I was hoping that maybe I could buy some of your samples to use for the opening, and naturally I'd post signs that your shop provided the hor d'oerves for the event. Some of the people who will be attending are quite wealthy - artists and illustrators who live in the area, and might be looking for caterers to use for their next events."

Andrea rolled her eyes. "I can't imagine--" she stopped short with a warning look from Josh, and MacKenzie watched the interplay with interest. Mr. Williams raised his eyebrows, his expression thoughtful.

"If you think your businesses could work together," he said, his attention mainly on the Taylor siblings. "That could potentially be a benefit for the mall. I might be able to convince the board that it's worth a trial period to see if you two can work out your differences with Ms. Jones here."

Josh nodded, glancing at MacKenzie before turning back to Mr. Williams. "I think we'd like the chance to do that, Sir. The grand opening seems like a perfect opportunity, as Ms. Jones said. Will you give us a month to see what we can work out long-term?"

The manager looked at Andrea for a long time, and then at MacKenzie, who smiled. Finally, he nodded.

"You have one month to prove to me your two stores can co-exist peacefully. Any complaints about either of your stores within that time period will leave me no choice but to cancel both of your contracts. Understood?"

MacKenzie's mouth fell open. "Sir?"

He turned to her and shrugged. "You chose to stick your neck out for them when the board is anxious for them to leave. So they're your responsibility now. I'm sorry, but that's the way the board will see it. I'd suggest you do whatever you can to not screw this up."

With one last look at all three of them, he turned and walked out the door.

"Well." Andrea crossed her arms over her chest. "I don't know what possessed either of you two to make a deal like that, but it looks like we'll both be looking for a new location at the end of the month, because I have no intention of cross-promoting our gourmet food with comic books. So congratulations to you both."

Josh shook his head. "You still don't get it, do you? We can't afford to move, Andrea. It'll be a few more years before we have enough profit coming in for things like that - we're still recovering from...before. If we lose this shop, we're done. Dad's not going to finance a new start for a venture he's been against all along, and we both put everything we had into turning this place around. So whether you like it or not, working with Kenzie's Comics is our best chance right now."

Rubbing her forehead, Andrea seemed to deflate. When she looked up, her hard stare locked on MacKenzie.

"Which samples did you want?" she asked, her tone cold, but resolute. MacKenzie handed her the list.

"I picked out five that would be appropriate, but I only need two. Whichever two are the easiest for you to replace will be fine, but I'd appreciate the least expensive as well. I'm running on very thin margins myself at the moment."

Andrea looked at the list, and then nodded. "I'll have Ella bring the boxes over tomorrow morning. What time are you opening?"

"Ten o'clock. What do I owe you?" MacKenzie held up her wallet.

Josh shifted, gaining her attention. "Don't worry about it," he said as Andrea nodded her acknowledgment, and then walked away. "Consider it our thanks for buying us some time. And for putting yourself on the line too - I know that wasn't your intent."

MacKenzie looked away. "Yeah. Well, there's always a twist, isn't there? I really think this could work though, if your sister will just--"

"Let me worry about her. You just concentrate on getting your store open, and we'll figure the rest out later, okay?"

When she looked up at him, he was smiling, and she returned the gesture.

"Okay. Thank you. I'll...um...see you later, then."

"Count on it." He winked, and she felt the heat rush into her cheeks as she turned and walked out as quickly as she could.

* * * * *

The next morning, MacKenzie was at the shop early, flitting through her final checklist and trying rather unsuccessfully to calm her nerves. Second-guessing herself for the fourth and fifth times in the last twenty-four hours, she moved the treat table, and then moved it back, and rearranged the free comic book table twice more until Trevor and Kevin finally showed up and shooed her away from the displays to make sure the extra inventory was neatly laid out on the back work table for quick re-stocking if necessary.

She knew in her head that she really shouldn't expect much. Considering about a hundred people had responded positively to a social media invite for the opening, she could safely assume that maybe twenty would actually follow through. It was just the way things worked. Still, in her heart, she wanted to believe that her store was something people would get excited about. And last night she'd announced that Taste the World would be providing gourmet snacks for the opening, which seemed to garner some interest as well.

There was a soft knock at the back door of the shop and she pulled it open, surprised to find Andrea herself standing there with a large white box in hand. Behind her Josh carried another box. MacKenzie motioned for them to come in.

"Good morning," she said, relieved that Andrea's scowl didn't seem quite as deep today. "There's a table out front - Kevin or Trevor can show you..." Her smile faded as three more people she didn't recognize filed in behind Josh, each with an equally large box in hand.

"Um..." she turned to ask Josh what was going on, but he'd already disappeared into the shop. After the last person was in, she closed the door and followed them, stopping short when she saw the tables she'd arranged so carefully being moved, re-covered and far more hor d'ouerves being placed on some sort of oddly-shaped platters than she'd originally asked for.

She started forward, panic and anger warring in her chest. She didn't even see Josh coming until he stepped in front of her, grabbing her upper arms with gentle, but firm hands.

"I know how this looks," he said, speaking slowly, as if to a child. "But believe me, she knows what she's doing. This is what she's good at, and if you just give it a chance, I think you'll see what I mean. Trust me?"

MacKenzie blinked, staring at him. Trust him? Really? She nearly laughed in his face.

"I didn't order all that," she said, trying to look around him, but blocked by his grip. "I can't pay for it either. And I need this opening to be about my books, my shop - your food is just a perk. Why would you do this to me? I thought we had an agreement?" She blinked faster, looking away as she tried not to cry. She should never have gone to them for help. If she'd just gone to the store and bought chips and brownies, her customers would never have known, and Taste the World would be moving out soon.

Her life was a nightmare.

She wrenched out of his grip and turned to go back to the stock room when Kevin ran up and touched her arm. The grin on his face was huge, and it just made her more angry. How could he possibly be okay with this?

"Kenzie, you gotta come see this," he said, taking her hand and pulling her back. "It's amazing. You're gonna freak out."

She certainly felt like freaking out. Preparing for the worst, she let him tug her past Josh, past Trevor, past the now smiling Andrea, which made her more nervous than ever.

The two tables she'd set up on either side of the room for free comics and treats were now angled off on either side of the door, creating an entry point to the store with a tiered display low in the center, and rising up and out to the ends of each table. The free issues were set toward the back in standing display racks, and she gasped as she walked through the center and finally turned to look at the tables from the front.

Brightly-colored platters in superhero shapes held bite-sized snacks, but not the ones she'd ordered. A black bat held what looked like square sugar cookies...with tiny comic book covers in frosting on the top. A red and blue triangle with a yellow S in the center held cupcakes...with tiny action figures stuck in red, white and blue frosting that matched many of those on the covers in the nearby displays. A tray shaped like a shield with silver stripes and stars held more cookies shaped like stars with yellow frosting, lanterns with green frosting and other iconic images from popular series.

Finally, a bright red platter held what appeared to be a rice-crispy cake shaped and decorated like a spider web and cut into bite-sized slivers with one lying invitingly on its side. Taste the World cards sat behind each platter telling customers what the treats were, and small stacks of business cards lay subtly back beside the comic books.

Speechless, MacKenzie looked up to see everyone watching her, and she shook her head.

"I--wow," she looked down at the table again. "This is...I mean, you must have been up all night. How...why?"

Andrea stepped forward. "Josh and I had a long talk last night after you left. I still don't like this - and I still think it's a bad idea to link our two shops together. But I told him we could use this as a test. I stayed up all night making these - not for you, but to make us look good. If we get at least one catering order from this, I'll try to be more open to whatever other cross-promotion suggestions you have. If not," she shrugged, the implication clear.

MacKenzie nodded. "You know I can't afford all this..."

"No charge," Andrea said, looking at her watch. "Now if we can dispense with the drama, it's nearly time for you to open your doors, and we need to get back to the kitchen. If you run out, send someone over. We have extras ready."

She turned, motioning to her staff to follow and they filed out the back after her, leaving MacKenzie with Kevin, Trevor and Josh, who moved closer with a slight smirk on his lips.

"Everything okay now?" he asked. MacKenzie just nodded,

still trying to process it all. "You should know that this wasn't my idea," he continued, nodding as she met his gaze. "I just talked her into cooperating. She's the one who decided to do the theme, and she spent a fair amount of time online last night getting ideas while her staff was baking. Give her a chance. She might come around yet."

He turned and left, and MacKenzie let out a big sigh, then looked at Kevin and Trevor. They both had huge smiles on their faces, and she couldn't help but smile back.

"This is really happening, isn't it?" she said. The guys nodded, and Kevin stepped up to give her a hug.

"You did it, Kenzie. Now what do you say we let those poor people in a little early, since they were kind enough to show up and wait in line. He grasped her shoulders and turned her around, and she gasped.

There was indeed a line of people waiting outside the door. And one of the catering staff from Taste the World was going down the line, passing out what looked like molded chocolates.

"Can this day get any better?" she murmured, taking the key out of her pocket.

"Only if you let those people in," Trevor answered with a laugh. "Let's get this party started!"

MacKenzie grinned as she unlocked the door and propped it open, personally greeting every person in line as they came into the shop. Josh came into view for just a few minutes, refilling the caterer's tray. As he turned to go back into his store, his eyes met hers for a brief moment, and he smiled.

MacKenzie smiled back, and tried to ignore that dangerous flutter in the region of her heart as she greeted the next customer.

Chapter 4

"That's a horrible idea," MacKenzie said, rubbing the side of her face with one hand. "Do you have any idea what that chocolate concoction will do to my comics when it splatters all over the place? And it will. You know it will. Kids are kids."

The grand opening of the store had been a great success - better than she could have expected, and Taste the World had landed several new contracts that day as well. Now, a week later, MacKenzie was meeting with Josh and Andrea to plan a display in front of their shops for the annual Go Green event at the mall, and suddenly, Andrea was full of ideas. Most of them were great.

The chocolate fountain flowing with white chocolate dyed green was not one of them.

"The chocolate won't splatter that bad," Andrea said, frustration raising her voice. "Can't you put your comics in those bags or something to protect them? We always do a fountain, and all the candy shops are doing one, so we really don't have a choice here. It's non-negotiable!"

"Even bags aren't going to keep that stuff out completely, and besides, when customers buy bagged comics, they want the bags to stay clean. We'd have to double-bag everything, and you have no idea how time-consuming that is. Besides, don't we have enough already with the green marshmallow squares and mudslide brownies and taffy and pudding shots and whatever else is on this list?" She held up a sheet of paper, shaking it slightly for emphasis.

Andrea shook her head, collapsing back in her chair with a dramatic noise, and then rising to her feet. She looked at Josh, then gestured toward MacKenzie. "That fountain is the centerpiece. It brings everything together, and if we don't have it, we don't have anything. Period. You like her - you talk some sense into her!"

She stomped out of the meeting room, and MacKenzie tossed the paper on the table.

"No. Just...no. This is not happening. No."

He cocked his head to the side, his expression thoughtful. "What if we put the fountain on a different table altogether? Would that work?"

"We're talking liquid candy here, Josh. And tiny, pint-sized fingers sneaking in for a dip, then coming over to thumb through a now unsalable comic book. How is it that you people can't understand that? And why is this fountain so damned important, anyways?"

He leaned forward, bracing both elbows on the table and rubbing his forehead.

"You heard Andrea. There's a candy shop, a pastry shop and that restaurant in the food court that serves healthy," he made air quotes with his fingers, "snacks. They all do chocolate fountains - it's just a thing. If we don't do one, we lose to the competition. It's that simple."

MacKenzie frowned, shaking her head. "This is a nightmare. If we could just each do separate tables--"

"Yeah, well, I tried to sell that to Mr. Williams already, and he refused. Like it or not, we're linked for good with that deal we agreed to when you opened, so we need to find a way around this problem, and fast."

He sat back again, staring thoughtfully at her for so long she started to squirm.

"What?" she finally asked, looking down at her shirt to make sure she hadn't spilled anything on it when Andrea had brought in some of the chocolate fountain sauce to sample, and half-hoping she had just to prove her point. Seeing nothing, she looked up at him again.

"Have dinner with me," he said, a challenge in his eyes. "Let's get out of here and see if we can get a different perspective on the problem."

She was already shaking her head. "That is not a good idea," she said, gathering the papers in front of her into a neat pile. She'd been steering clear of Josh as much as possible since her store had opened, not wanting to be tempted by something she couldn't have, and shouldn't want anyway. Dinner was easily as bad an idea as the chocolate fountain.

"Why not? Scared?" The knowing look in his eyes irritated her, and she glared back as she rose from her chair.

"Of course not," she lied, grabbing her papers. "I have other plans, but we can talk about this again tomorrow. I'll--"

"That's not what Kevin said when I saw him earlier today."

She turned back with a frown. "You talked to Kevin? About me?" As soon as the words were out of her mouth, she would have given anything to take them back. Could she sound any more paranoid?

He nodded, getting up and moving to stand in front of her.

His closeness was both intimidating and intoxicating, but she didn't dare back away, or he'd know he made her nervous.

Though by the look in his eyes, he was already far too aware of that inconvenient fact.

"We had a nice conversation, actually. He mentioned that you weren't doing anything tonight. He also mentioned that you like Thai food. As luck would have it, I like Thai food too, so we should go eat. Together. Think of it as being efficient."

She rolled her eyes at him. "But what would your parents think? Or Andrea, for that matter? Aren't you supposed to stay away from smart girls like me?"

"You're not being particularly smart at the moment, and we need that fountain. He's got my blessing - now go!"

MacKenzie jumped at Andrea's voice from the other end of the room, turning just in time to catch a rare grin from the woman before she left again just as quickly. Looking back at Josh, the insufferable lout was smiling wide.

"That is a once-in-a-lifetime endorsement," he said, pointing at the empty doorway. "We'd both be fools not to take advantage of it."

MacKenzie's stomach chose just that moment to gurgle its approval, garnering a laugh from her hopeful dinner companion.

"Come on, Kenzie. It's just dinner. We both know you want to. What could it hurt?"

She sighed, mentally listing all the myriads of ways dinner with Josh was a really bad idea, not the least of which was the possibility of eventually getting her heart broken. But it wasn't going to go that far. It was just dinner, and she was a big girl who had managed to keep things professional with this man aside from one moment that she'd definitely forgotten all about.

She could do this.

"Fine," she said, giving in against her better judgment. "Let me get my coat and tell Kevin I'm leaving. I'll meet you out back."

* * * * *

Pleasantly surprised when MacKenzie actually came out the back door of the mall, Josh smiled.

"I kind of thought you'd back out on me," he said, walking toward his car. When she didn't fall into step beside him, he turned back to see her still standing several feet away.

"I'm over there," she said, pointing in the other direction. "Where did you want to meet?"

He raised an eyebrow. "There's no point in taking two cars - I can bring you back afterwards." It was cute how nervous she was, but did she seriously think he'd jump her in the car? Last time they'd had a great conversation...

And then you nearly kissed her, you idiot.

"That's okay." Her voice was calm. Reasonable. "It'll be easier to just drive myself home afterwards. More efficient, and I know how you like that."

He laughed. Of course she would throw his own words back at him. "Touché. How about Thai Gardens on Sixth? Will that work?"

She nodded. "Absolutely. See you there in a few minutes." Turning on her heel, she strode purposefully across the parking lot and got in her car - a sporty little blue sedan of some sort. He watched her pull out of the lot and then went to his SUV, looking forward to what promised to be a very entertaining evening.

The restaurant was crowded, but they were able to get a table way back in the corner by the kitchen. It was surprisingly cozy, and Josh enjoyed the way his knees brushed against MacKenzie's when she moved.

He especially enjoyed the way she blushed when it happened.

After they'd each ordered the buffet and filled a plate, she took a sip of her water and picked up her fork.

"I know you wanted to come here because there's a chocolate fountain on the dessert buffet," she said, glancing over at the offending item. "Do you see any books in this place?"

He gave her that one. "No, but do you see chocolate everywhere? Aside from the immediate area around the fountain, I mean."

"No, but there are staff constantly cleaning here. And food everywhere. Any one of the children eating here could have sticky fingers from that fountain. And again, no books."

Josh ate a few bites, trying to think of another way to make his point. Except there really wasn't one. She was right - having her books anywhere near the chocolate fountain was asking for trouble. Unless...

"What about this," he said, looking into her eyes. "We have some mall chain and posts in the back room, so we can make it like a buffet table. Shoppers come in one end to browse your books, and then as they move through, they get to our sweets and finally the chocolate fountain..." he held a hand up and raised his eyebrows when she opened her mouth to interrupt. "The fountain at the end of the line, with one of our staff people doing all of the dipping and serving, and making sure people don't go backwards through the line."

He paused, waiting for her to object. He took it as a good sign when she didn't.

"I'll even have another one of our staff handing out wet wipes just to make sure. Can you live with that?"

She was considering it, which was more than she'd done with any of his earlier suggestions. He decided to sweeten the pot a bit.

"You think about it," he said, putting his napkin on the table. "I'll be right back."

He went to the dessert table and filled a plate with a large strawberry, a big marshmallow and a shortbread cookie dipped in the chocolate fountain, carrying it back to the table and setting it between them.

"You don't seriously think--"

He held up a chocolate covered cookie, interrupting her.

"Imagine this cookie shaped like the Hulk. Or Swamp Thing. Or Green Lantern. Dripping with green chocolate." He held it in front of her mouth, one hand underneath to catch any drips. "Kids will love it. Their favorite superhero, dipped in green slime."

She rolled her eyes, but took a bite, her expression lightening a bit as she chewed.

"We can do marshmallows too - like this one." He popped the remainder of the cookie into his own mouth as she watched with wide eyes, and then held out a chocolate-sauced marshmallow dipped in graham cracker crumbs for her to try. She locked eyes with him as she took a big bite, leaving only a small piece for him to finish and a tantalizing drip of chocolate at the corner of her mouth.

He swiped it off with his finger, putting it in his own mouth as she slowly finished her part of the treat.

The air seemed to grow thicker, the noise around them quieter as he held the strawberry out for her to taste.

"We won't have fruit," he said, all too aware that his voice had gone husky and low. "But no one can resist chocolate and strawberries."

From the look in her eyes as she bit into the sweet berry, she was just as affected by the moment as he was, and it took every ounce of strength he had not to move to her side and share the last bite up close and in person. He leaned closer, drowning in those big blue eyes and dying to taste those sweet lips. His heart beat faster, and for a second, he thought she was leaning toward him too.

"You enjoyed your dinner?"

The waiter's cheerful voice cut through the cloudy haze, and MacKenzie's eyes widened just before she looked away. Josh looked up too, scowling at the man who held out a small tray with their bill.

"Y-Yes, thank you," MacKenzie said, flashing the man a smile and reaching for the tray. Josh snatched it away, earning a frown.

"What's my half?" MacKenzie asked, getting her wallet out of her purse. Josh shook his head.

"My treat," he said, retrieving his own wallet. "It's a business expense." He laid a card on the tray with a smile.

MacKenzie laid her card with his, raising her eyebrows. "Right. Which means I get to claim half of it. You wouldn't take a deduction away from a fledgling comic book shop, would you?"

He laughed, and sat back in his chair. "I guess I can't argue with logic like that, can I? But I'm curious. When was the last time you let a man buy you dinner?"

Her eyes sparkled with mischief. "When was the last time you let a woman buy you dinner?"

"Are you offering?" He winked, enjoying the way her cheeks turned pink at the suggestion. "Because that would be a new one for me, but I'm completely open to the idea. As long as it's not business, of course."

"How sad," MacKenzie said as the waiter brought back their cards and two receipts. She stood, slinging her purse strap over her shoulder.

Josh got to his feet as well. "Why do you say that?" He followed her to the door, enjoying the view as her hips swayed slightly. Smart and good-looking really was a lethal combination.

MacKenzie held the door open for him as he followed her out, and then shrugged.

"You've undoubtedly dated a lot of women. And not one of them ever bothered to pick up the check. You don't think that's sad? Don't you ever feel like you're being used for your money?"

He walked with her to her car, noting she didn't object. "Sometimes," he said, reaching for the handle and pulling the door open for her after she unlocked it. "But most of the time, it's my pleasure to buy dinner for a female companion. It's a guy thing. We may not hunt anymore, but we take care of..."

He knew the moment the words were out that MacKenzie would take exception if he finished the sentence. She was already looking at him with that sharp, electric stare that said he was in trouble.

"Oh please," she said, her tone saccharine-sweet. "Don't stop now. I'm dying to hear the rest of that statement."

He laughed. He couldn't help it. She gave him an indulgent smile in return, waiting patiently between the car and the open door as he got himself together.

"You really are something," he said, his hands resting between hers on top of the fiberglass between them. "I can never let my guard down with you around, can I?"

Her smile faded and she looked down, sliding into the driver's seat. "I do tend to have that affect on people. Have a good night, Josh. I'll stop by and finalize the details with Andrea tomorrow." She pulled at the door, looking pointedly at his hands. He didn't want to let go, but sensed that pushing her now would probably just result in sore fingers, so he did, taking a step back as she started the engine and drove off into the night.

He watched until her tail lights disappeared, and then went to his own vehicle, replaying the last few minutes of conversation over in his head. He'd been teasing, of course, but obviously she'd taken it more seriously than he'd intended.

As he drove home, he considered what he could do to make it up to her. Something that would get them back to where they'd been in that moment before the damn waiter had interrupted their interlude.

Because caveman that he was, he was determined to taste that smart mouth at least once. Though he suspected once would never actually be enough.

Chapter 5

"ey Kev," MacKenzie said the next morning, standing in front of Kevin's desk. "Wanna get up and stretch your legs a bit?"

He looked up from the screen, a dubious expression under the jet black shock of hair that fell across one side of his face. He was attractive in a tall, slender, rock-star/artist sort of way, and when they'd first met, she might have had a little crush on the guy. That had dissipated quickly, but their friendship had grown strong, and while the romantic element had never surfaced again, his writing and her illustrations were the perfect pairing.

"Why would I want to do that? And more importantly, why would you want me to? I smell a conspiracy here..."

She blinked innocently. "You think I have an ulterior motive? I was merely offering you a chance to get out of the office for a little while. But if you don't want to come with..."

She shrugged, turning away with the best nonchalant look she could manage. After the fiasco with Josh last night, she wanted more of a buffer at their meeting this morning than just Andrea.

Kevin pushed his chair back with a sigh. "I don't know what you're up to, Kenz, but I suspect you're going to owe me when this is done. So where are we going?"

"Not far," she said with a coy smile, leading him out of the shop. When she opened the door to Taste the World, he rolled his eyes.

"You're sick, you know that?" He kept his voice low, winking at the hostess behind the marble bar with a smile.

"She's way too young for you, Kev. Don't even think about it." She stopped at the doorway to the back offices.

"Josh is expecting us - can we go back?"

The hostess nodded. "They're waiting for you in the conference room."

MacKenzie went through the door and around the corner, holding the conference room door open for Kevin. She was all too aware of the two people already at the table staring at her companion. Good. Make 'em wonder.

The introductions didn't take long, though MacKenzie noted the few extra seconds Kevin and Andrea seemed to...linger over a handshake. It was probably just her imagination, and she forced herself to focus as she leaned forward, ignored Josh and addressed Andrea directly.

"Did Josh tell you what the new plan we agreed on was?"

Andrea nodded, her eyes flicking briefly over to Kevin.

"It sounds good to me. We have to have the display ready first thing tomorrow morning - does tonight after closing work for set-up for you? Or we could do it in the morning...we'll be here around four a.m. to make the snacks."

MacKenzie looked at Kevin. "Want to stay late with me tonight?" He shrugged, and she took that as about as close to a yes as she was going to get. "We can do the comic shop's portion tonight, and then you guys can fill in with the snacks tomorrow morning, if that's okay with everyone. The mall opens at ten, so I'll be here at nine to help finish up."

Kevin leaned forward. "Actually, I'd rather come in early Kenzie, if that's okay with you. I can set the tables up before I leave though, so you can start on stuff tonight. I can finish in the morning."

"I can help tonight," Josh said, and MacKenzie swiveled her chair to look at him as he continued. "And then Kevin can help Andrea in the morning."

His expression was bland, almost bored, and she almost wondered if he'd actually spoken or if she was just hearing things. She must be more tired than she thought.

Not tired enough to fall into that trap, thank goodness.

"Thanks, but that's really not necessary," she said with her own cool, professional smile. "I can handle most of it tonight myself, and I'm sure Kevin can finish it off in the morning."

"Nonsense," he said, only his eyes relaying a personal challenge just for her. "I can help set up the tables and put the traffic chain in place so Kevin doesn't have to stay late. It makes sense, don't you think, since we're kind of forced to work on this together?"

Kevin nodded. "That works better for me. I'd be happy to be the muscle for Andrea in the morning." He glanced at her, and MacKenzie barely resisted the urge to grin. From the look on Andrea's face, she wasn't going to let him get away with the implication that she needed help.

"You can just worry about your books, writer-boy. I can take care of the food myself." She arched a brow, and MacKenzie looked at Kevin, anxious to hear his response.

He actually laughed, causing Andrea's arched brow to fall.

"Whatever you say, baker-girl," he said, the sarcasm impossible to miss. "I'll be here bright and early, so if you end up in over your dough, you know where to find me."

Andrea started to retort, but Josh interrupted.

"So it's settled then. Kevin and I will be available whenever you two superwomen decide you need something heavy carried around or moved repeatedly from one area to the next. Until then, we'll watch quietly from the sidelines at the times we've chosen. I think that's all we need to discuss, right Kevin?"

The other man stood, grinning as he nodded. "That about sums it up, I think. Hey man, wanna go grab some coffee? Or is it safe to leave these two alone?"

Josh chuckled. "I think it's safe enough for now. Being mad at us should keep them from killing each other until they get tired of complaining about how stupid and stubborn we are." The two men shared a laugh as they walked out, leaving MacKenzie to stare across the table at Andrea, who looked just as shell-shocked as she felt.

"Did they just...?" she said.

Andrea nodded. "Make all the decisions and then just walk out, like antiquated cavemen? Yes."

"Huh." MacKenzie rubbed her forehead, not sure what to do next.

"Yeah." Andrea sighed, pushing back her chair. "I guess it's time to get back to work then."

"I guess so." MacKenzie stood up, thinking that this was the most civil conversation she'd had with Josh's sister since they met.

Damn men.

"I'll...um...see you tomorrow then."

"Yep." Andrea headed for the back door of the conference room, and MacKenzie went out the front, walking quickly through the store, out to the mall and back into the relative sanity of her comic book shop.

Trevor was behind the counter, reading a copy of the latest Action Comics. She stopped, cocking her head to the side until he looked up and met her gaze. His eyes widened for a moment, as if he recognized something, and then narrowed before he shook his head and looked back down at the page he'd been reading.

"Yes, all men are jerks. No, we have no idea why."

She laughed. "How did you know what I was going to ask?"

He shrugged. "It's the one question women always want to know the answer to, and you had that look."

"What look? There's a look for that?" She frowned, wishing she had a mirror.

He just waved her off. "Be gone, boss! I'm researching the inventory."

"You're lucky I like you," she said, catching a smirk on his face as she went past him into the back office and sat down behind her desk. She knew she should finalize the Go Green booth design now that they had a plan, but she didn't even want to think about it just then.

Instead, she pulled out her sketches of the latest Charade panels. Drawing calmed her, centered her mind. She'd just work on one more page before getting back to the business of...well, business. And annoying cavemen.

* * * * *

Josh grinned at Kevin's chuckle as they walked out of the shop and down the mall corridor.

"That was classic, man," the writer said, hands shoved in the pockets of his jeans. "I don't think either of the girls knew what to do after that."

"It does catch 'em off guard when we actually make decisions. Probably because we just don't care enough to say anything most of the time, so when we do, they don't know what to do. And between you and me," he leaned in conspiratorially. "I think they like it when we just decide to help, whether they want it or not. I mean, obviously they don't need us ordering them around all the time, but helping 'em cart heavy stuff and do the grunt work? I think those animal instincts come into play and they secretly like letting us be guys. Besides, it gives them another reason to order us around - and we all know they love to do that."

Kevin shook his head, laughing as they stopped at a coffee kiosk. "You'd better not let Kenzie hear you talking like that, or she'll kick you to the curb faster than you can blink."

Josh shrugged. "Have you been working together long?"

"A few years," Kevin said as they started back to their end of the mall. "We met at a party in college, thought we might date but that didn't really work out. We were sharing work one day, you know, just casually, and one of her drawings fit perfectly with this story I'd started. That's when we started working together, and we've been partners ever since."

Josh pictured MacKenzie bent over a table sketching, and he liked the image. Would she ever let him watch her at work, he wondered?

"Why didn't the couple thing work out for you two, if you don't mind my asking?"

"Gotta have chemistry, man. Kenzie's like a sister to me. And she feels the same way about me. We just weren't feelin' it, you know?"

Josh nodded, glancing sideways at Kevin as they walked. "So she's not currently seeing anyone?"

Kevin laughed. "You're kidding, right? She's too busy telling herself she shouldn't be seeing you to focus on anyone else." They were nearing the shops, and Kevin stopped, turning to look Josh in the eye.

"Look man. She doesn't tell me everything, but I know her pretty well. And she's got the hots for you, but for some reason, you've got her running scared. My advice is either to tell her how you feel and go for broke, or stay away from her. She's already got enough going on that she doesn't need to worry about where she stands with you on top of everything else. Understand?"

"Yeah," Josh said, catching sight of MacKenzie just inside her store. When she looked up and saw him, she quickly turned and walked away from the window. "Yeah, I hear you. Thanks."

Kevin headed into the comic shop and Josh went back to his office. He wasn't so sure that pushing the matter was going to help his cause with Kenzie, but he definitely needed to decide whether he really wanted to subject her to his family and his life, or if it would be better for her if he just stayed away. It wasn't fair to keep teasing her along if he had no intention of following through.

The odds of her surviving any kind of courtship with him were virtually none, unless he was willing to stand up for her - something he had failed to do with all of his past girlfriends, to his discredit. Standing against his parents...he knew she couldn't understand, but it was a life-altering thing. One that he could never take back.

Andrea appeared in the doorway and he smiled at her, motioning for her to come in.

"So," she said, taking a seat in front of his desk. "I guess you really like her, right?"

Josh frowned. "Who?" Surely she couldn't read his mind, and he knew he hadn't been thinking out loud.

Andrea rolled her eyes. "Comic-shop girl? MacKenzie Jones? The woman you wouldn't take no from earlier today? Come on, Josh. It would be obvious to a blind person that you two are attracted to each other."

He shrugged. "That doesn't mean anything's going to happen between us." Rubbing his face with his hands, he sighed. "Actually, it would probably be better if someone else helped her tonight. Do you think one of the caterers would stay late?"

She sat back in her chair, her expression thoughtful. "You sure you want to do that? Because I got the impression--"

"I'm sure. I thought maybe it could work, but I've never been able to go against the family, and I'm honestly not sure I could this time either. She doesn't deserve to be put through all that just so I can find out."

"Something tells me that girl can take care of herself, brother-dear, but if you want to play it safe, I understand. I'll see if Todd can stay. Why don't you go ahead and get out of here early? I can hold down the fort until closing."

He hesitated until he realized she was trying to make sure he didn't back down now that the decision had been made.

"Okay. I'll see you tomorrow then."

They both stood, and he followed her through the kitchen to the back door, where she gave him a quick hug.

"You're doing the right thing," she whispered in his ear before he left. As he walked to the car, he couldn't help but feel like he was doing exactly the wrong thing, even if it was for the right reasons.

Chapter 6

After the mall closed, MacKenzie tried to mentally prepare herself to spend time with Josh as she put together a box with table coverings, a few figures, and the comic books she'd double-bagged just in case. Picking it up, she carried it through the store and pushed the door into the mall open with a shoulder, careful to keep her expression neutral. Further down the corridor there were a few others setting up displays as well, though it looked like the majority of shopkeepers had opted for an early morning start instead.

Four folding tables had been delivered by mall maintenance, two in front of each shop. The door to Taste the World was propped open, and as she set the box on one of the tables, a caterer she sort of recognized came out carrying a metal post with a weighted base and some chain.

He smiled and nodded at her, setting the items down and wiping his hands on his pants before holding one out to her.

"Todd Morgan," he said, his grip firm but not bone-crushing as she shook his hand. "Josh had to leave early, so I offered to help instead. If that's okay with you."

Yes! No! Yes! She returned his smile with a quick nod, ignoring the warring emotions taking over her head. Did Josh really have something else to do? Or was he avoiding her after making such a big deal of helping tonight?

Could she be any more pathetic for even caring?

"I appreciate that," she said, trying to get a hold of herself. "If you want to get the rest of the posts, I'll arrange the tables and we can put the chain up. I should be able to take it from there."

He nodded. "More kid-blockers, coming right up." With a friendly grin he disappeared back into the store, and MacKenzie blew out a long breath. It was good Josh wasn't here. She could concentrate, get everything done and get a good night's sleep without being distracted. Definitely for the best.

She pulled the tables into the curved shape they'd agreed on, placing rigid wooden platforms at the outer edges to block the gaps and round the corners. There was a milk crate sitting just outside the door to the catering shop with light green linens, napkins and some empty platters, so she flipped the tablecloths out over the tables as Todd set up the perimeter chains. Arranging her comic-themed coverings diagonally over the green linens, she stepped back to look, and then glanced at Todd, eyebrows raised.

"I like it," he said, standing beside her with his arms crossed. "Andrea said everything in the crate needs to fit with your stuff. If you can't find room, she'll figure it out tomorrow with Kevin." He made a show of rolling his eyes, and she laughed. Apparently she wasn't the only one Andrea liked to boss around.

"I'm sure I can figure something out," she said. "You can take off if you want. The heavy lifting is done, and it might take me awhile to come up with a table arrangement I like. Thanks for your help though - I appreciate it."

He tipped his head to the side. "Anytime - it was no problem at all. I'll see you around."

He went into the store and she heard the lock click on the doors as she started setting out book displays and platters. A few minutes later, the lights dimmed behind the glass. As she worked alone, the tension from the day dissipated and it wasn't long before she stood back behind the chain again to admire her work.

On her two tables, standing displays held a few copies of the latest and most popular issues, including a few foodie-themed comics toward the catering tables. Graphic novels lay haphazardly between platters that would hold bite-sized treats come tomorrow morning, and business cards for both shops were scattered liberally around it all. A few collectibles in boxes sat at the back of the table between the book displays, in hopes that only adult arms would be long enough to reach.

There was a gradual shift to the food end of the tables, where she'd laid out the napkins, plastic ware and more platters, leaving space for the dreaded chocolate fountain at the end.

She'd never admit it to either of the Taylors, but it was going to be a nice finish for their table. As long as the staff was vigilant about watching for sticky hands and errant sauce.

Thinking about the smooth melted chocolate made her body warm as she remembered Josh feeding her chocolate covered bites the other night. Right from his hand. The way he'd looked into her eyes, as if he could read her thoughts.

The way he'd almost kissed her. And the way she'd wanted him to.

Shaking it off, she put the milk crate and her empty box underneath the tables and went back into her shop, locking the door behind her. She inhaled deeply as the scent of fresh comic books hit her nose, her eyes closing for just a second as the joy of the moment, standing there in her very own store, surrounded by the things she loved gave her one of those warm, fuzzy feelings everyone always went on about. Cliché for a reason, she acknowledged as she opened her eyes and walked through to the back, flipping the lights off as she passed the switch. Her stomach rumbled, and she pulled on her jacket, tossing her bag over one shoulder on her way to the door. She'd pick something up for dinner on the way home. But not Thai food.

As she went out the back door of the mall, her heart sped up when she noticed a tall figure leaning against the driver's side door of her car. Fumbling around in the back pocket of her purse, she grabbed the can of pepper spray kept there for emergencies, and held it out in front of her as she slowly approached.

"Step away from the car, please," she said in a loud, confident tone that carried across the lot. "I have pepper spray, and I'll use it if I have to."

A deep, familiar chuckle wafted toward her on the breeze as the figure straightened, holding both hands up in submission as he took a few steps away from the car and into the pool of light from a nearby streetlamp.

"Easy there, tiger," Josh said, his amused expression becoming clear as she drew closer. Letting her arms drop, she shook her head, stowing the pepper spray again.

"Why are you here?" she asked, not entirely sure she wanted to know the answer. He dropped his hands and came closer.

Too close.

She started to step back, but he reached out, gently grasping her upper arms to hold her in place.

"I tried to stay away," he said, his tone serious. "And if you're smart, you'll tell me to leave you alone, though I'll be perfectly honest - I'm not sure I can. There's just something about you…" he raised one hand to caress the side of her face, his fingers trailing lightly down over the side of her neck.

She looked down at his chest, trying not to tremble at his touch. This was it. She had to choose whether to let him in and probably get hurt, or keep him out and do her best to forget that she had feelings for him.

Walking away was the smart thing to do. And she was nothing if not smart.

He coaxed her to look up with his hand, and she saw the same angst that must be in her eyes reflected in his.

"This is a really bad idea," she murmured. He gave her a slight nod.

"I think we've established that pretty well at this point." He waited another heartbeat, and then took a step back. "So we're going to be smart then, right?" His hand slipped away from her skin, leaving her bereft of his warmth.

She could do this. She could get in her car, buy herself dinner and go home. Maybe she'd cry herself to sleep, but maybe not. They hadn't even kissed, for crying out loud.

He nodded again at her silence and turned to walk away.

"No," she whispered, willing him to stop. But he didn't, and an overwhelming sense of panic shot through her, made her take a step forward, and then another until she was running after him.

He turned at the sound of her footsteps and opened his arms, gathering her close as she reached him.

When his lips touched hers, it was quite possibly the most

right thing she'd felt in a long, long time.

* * * * *

Warm, soft, and minty, Kenzie's kiss was every bit as addictive as Josh had dared to expect. He breathed her in, feasting on her lips as if he hadn't eaten in days. Pulling her body tighter against him, he reveled in the way she kissed him back, as if she'd been starving too.

For him.

A low, gurgling noise intruded on the moment, and he reluctantly released his grip just a little as Kenzie pulled back. Opening her eyes, she gave him a sheepish grin.

"Sorry. I was going to pick up dinner on the way home, but sort of got distracted..."

It took him another second or two to realize that the noise he'd heard was her stomach rumbling...and then it did again.

He laughed, tugging her closer again. "Well, we have two options, since I'm not even close to ready to say goodnight. You can let me buy you dinner, or you can offer to buy me dinner. Lady's choice, of course."

There was a mischievous twinkle in her eye, and he knew he'd missed something. Again.

"What, no option for us to each buy our own dinner?" She shook her head, clicking her tongue at him. "For shame, Mr. Taylor. I fear the concept of equality is lost on you."

He shrugged, thankful for the teasing note in her voice. "You might be right, unfortunately. It just seems so...cold that way, don't you think? More professional than personal? And believe me, the plans I have for you are anything but professional at the moment."

She laughed. "In that case, I'll buy you dinner. I wouldn't want you to think I was taking advantage of you or anything."

He leaned down to kiss her again, a quick, soft touch. "Honey, you can take advantage of me anytime you want. Now, where do you want to eat?"

She thought about it for a moment. "Let's go to that Irish pub just up the street, if you don't mind walking. They have an excellent, if ironic, French Dip I really like."

He took her hand, lacing his fingers with hers as they started to walk. "Good choice. Don't tell my sister, but I like their nachos better than hers."

Kenzie gasped, slapping her free hand to her chest in mock surprise.

"Sacrilege! But thank you. Now I can redirect her anger at you the next time she gets mad at me for something."

He chuckled, happy beyond measure in that moment though he knew it wouldn't always be this easy. But for now, he just wanted to enjoy the moment, and glancing at Kenzie's smile as they walked, he knew she did too.

"You know, that just might work." He squeezed her hand, and she squeezed his back as he pulled the door to the pub open for her.

Inexplicably nervous, he followed her to a table near the window, feeling much like his younger self on a first date. They sat down and placed their orders, and Josh couldn't think of a thing to say.

Neither could Kenzie, judging by her silence.

Mentally chastising himself for reverting to awkward-teen-mode, he leaned forward and took her hand across the table.

"So...why a comic book store?" he asked, genuinely curious.

She looked down at their joined hands, tilting her head to the side in a way that made him want to caress the side of her neck.

"I've always loved comic books. My dad bought me my first one when I was just a little girl, and I was just so fascinated by the bright colors and artwork - back then, they were still on newsprint, of course. I loved reading too, and I started drawing pictures for the stories in my books...I mean, literally in my books, which did not make my mom happy." She laughed, pulling her hand away so the server could set their plates down. "By the time I got to high school, I knew I wanted to be a comic book artist someday, much to my parent's chagrin. They convinced me to get a business degree along with my art degree, convinced I'd starve without something to fall back on. And voila! A comic book store is born." She picked up her sandwich. "What about you? Did you always want to run a catering business?"

Josh shook his head and swallowed. "Nope. But I love to eat, and the guy Andrea hired to do the books left both her and their catering business high and dry - taking plenty of money he'd skimmed with him. My parents put up the capitol to get the business back on its feet, with the caveat that I manage the financials and help with the overall company decisions. So here I am. We're doing our best to make a comeback, but it's slow going."

Kenzie nodded. "So you don't cook at all then? What did you do before this?"

"I do cook. I can make anything that has instructions for the microwave on it." He looked down at his plate. "And before Taste the World, I worked for my dad's firm." It always sounded impressive when he told people who were familiar with his father, but for some reason, with Kenzie, it seemed…juvenile.

If she thought so, she didn't show it. Her eyebrows rose, interest on her face.

"Oh really? What kind of a firm? A big one, I'm guessing." she grinned, her gentle eyes teasing. So why did he suddenly feel defensive?

Ignoring his instincts, he returned her smile. "He deals in real estate law and investments. My job was researching tax liens, buying property when it was a good deal, and selling it for a profit…" He stopped as her smile faded, and she leaned back in her chair. "What's wrong?"

She shook her head, crossing her arms over her chest and looking out the dark window.

"Taylor Investments. Of course. I should have known." She looked at him again, scrutinizing his face. "You look like him, now that I think about it. Thank God you didn't inherit that whole soul-sucking reaper vibe he carries around with him. I bet you were glad to leave."

Josh put his fork down, frowning. "He can be a hard-ass, sure, but he's not the devil, if that's what you're implying. And I liked working there. Made a lot of money that way."

She leaned forward slightly. "Your father's company is the reason my parents lost their house, and their good credit - and it was all due to a paperwork mix-up at the tax office that Taylor Investments grabbed and ran with. And do you know what your father said to me when I went to his office to explain what happened, and get the problem cleared up?"

Josh sighed, tossing his napkin on the table. "I'm betting you're going to tell me."

"He told me that he didn't believe me, even when I showed

him the correct papers, and explained what happened. He said he didn't care that my parents had no where else to go, or that they'd be on the street, so long as he made his money. And then he had security escort me out of the building."

"I'm sorry," Josh said, knowing it wasn't going to help, but needing to say it anyway. "Unfortunately, there are a lot of people who come in claiming all sorts of things to try to get their properties back, and I understand how hard it must be--"

MacKenzie raised her eyebrows, and he stopped. Her eyes flared with fire, and not the kind he'd been hoping to see.

"What's the worst thing that happens to you if you lose your place, Josh? You go move in with dear old dad for awhile? Or your sister, maybe? Maybe one of your rich friends. No matter what happens, you have a place to stay, and probably not just a couch to sleep on either. Your dad's company causes a lot of heartache. Period. You can't justify that."

He shook his head, holding up a hand. "Now wait a minute. Most of those people would lose their houses anyway. If not to Taylor Investments, then to the bank and foreclosure. Someone's going to make money off of it - if not companies like my dad's, then the bank, or someone else. It's the way things work, MacKenzie. You don't pay your debts, you lose your stuff. And someone has to manage those properties when that happens."

She shook her head, refusing to look him in the eye as she stood and put her purse over her shoulder.

"Thank you for dinner, but I have to go," she said, her voice quiet. "I'll see you around."

"Kenzie, wait." He tossed a couple large bills on the table and followed her out the door, his head spinning at how quickly the night had gone so wrong. Reaching the sidewalk, he jogged to catch up as she walked quickly back to the mall parking lot.

"I'm not my dad, you know," he said, striding easily beside her.

She shrugged, not bothering to turn her head. "No, you're not. But you think like he does. If you don't see anything wrong with the way he makes his money, that's a problem for me."

He nodded, watching as she unlocked her car door and pulled it open. Holding it while she slid behind the wheel, he bent down, annoyed that she still wouldn't look at him.

"Kenzie." She finally met his gaze, the cool hurt in her eyes wounding his soul. "You know we're not always going to agree on everything, right?"

"Yes." She looked down at her hands, and then back at him. "But our worlds are very different. Maybe too different, like you said before. It's probably better if we just--"

He put a hand over her lips, shaking his head. "Don't. We'll figure it out, just don't write this off yet. Please."

She turned her head away and started the car. "I need to go."

He stood, hesitating for one more long moment before he closed the door. His chest felt tight as she drove away, and he had no idea how to bridge this new chasm between them.

Chapter 7

MacKenzie got to the store late the next morning, thankful to see Andrea, Kevin and a host of other catering staff out front putting the final touches on the tables. Peering out through her store window, she was relieved that Josh didn't seem to be around, at least not yet.

She'd spent half the night trying to figure out why he couldn't see why she was so upset with his father's business ethics, and the other half of the night trying to see things from his point of view. Neither had been particularly successful, and now she was just tired, heartsick and crabby. Her head hurt, and she was in no mood to deal with customers, so she was hoping she could talk Kevin into working the store counter while Trevor worked the Go Green booth, allowing her to hide in the back at least until she felt better.

A couple cups of coffee might be a good place to start.

"Kenzie! I'm glad you're here." Andrea actually smiled at her as she bustled forward. She carried a tray of small green cookies shaped like shamrocks, and held it out to MacKenzie as she drew nearer.

"You have to taste these - they're perfect, and it was Kevin's recipe, if you can believe that. I'm going to scatter them through the display, if you don't mind."

MacKenzie took one and nodded. "It's fine with me. Do whatever you want. Everything looks great." She attempted a smile, but knew it fell short when Andrea's brows drew together.

"What's wrong?" she asked, setting the cookie tray on the table and leaning closer. "You don't look so good. Actually, you look like you've been up all night."

It was odd and a little disconcerting when MacKenzie felt Josh come up behind her. A quick peek at her reflection in the store window confirmed it.

She shook her head. "I was just up late, is all. Had a lot on my mind. I'm actually going to see if--"

Andrea looked past Mackenzie, eyes narrowed. "This is your fault, isn't it? I should have known. We can't afford to blow this day, brother-dear, and look at her. She can barely keep her eyes open!"

Grabbing MacKenzie's shoulders, Andrea spun her around before she could protest, putting her face-to-face with the one person she'd most like to avoid in the entire universe at that second.

Her gaze collided with his for a long second before she looked away. The wealth of emotions she felt in that moment were almost too much to process.

She should never have kissed him.

"I'm fine," she said, shrugging out of Andrea's hold. An electric hum filled the air just then, and the manager's voice floated over the loudspeaker.

"May I have your attention please. The Go Green shopping event is now officially open! Shoppers, don't forget to vote for your favorite booth at the customer service counter before you leave. Thank you for shopping with us."

MacKenzie turned to Kevin, standing behind the table. "Can you hang out here for a few minutes while I find Trevor? And maybe work the counter inside today?"

He shook his head. "Sorry Kenz. I can stay here for a few minutes, but I've got a meeting in an hour I can't miss."

"Okay." She sighed, then changed course. If she had to work, she might as well be out here where the action was, rather than falling asleep inside. "I'm just going to run get a big cup of coffee, and I'll be right back."

"I'll come with you." Josh fell into step beside her as she walked down the mall, dodging moms and kids and teenage packs along the way. She got all the way to the kiosk and up to the counter, placed her order, and realized as she patted her pockets that she'd left her wallet back at the shop.

"Damn it." She was just about to explain when two bills slid across the counter.

"Make that a double," he said to the barista. "My treat."

MacKenzie wanted to argue, and she also wanted to smack that silly lovestruck smile off the barista's face. She needed that coffee though, dammit, and when he placed the tall, steaming cup into her hands, years of conditioning couldn't be overridden.

"Thank you," she said, taking a sip of the hot liquid. The bemused smile he gave her told her he knew just how much she wanted to throw it in his face, and also that she wouldn't.

Annoying, arrogant bastard.

She rolled her eyes and turned on her heel, heading back to the shop as fast as she could, only to stop short when she saw Kevin take one of Andrea's hands and raise it to his lips in a gallant kiss. MacKenzie held her breath, waiting for the fireworks to start. What did he think he was doing?

But there was no yelling. No slap in the face. Nothing at all except a bright red blush on Andrea's cheeks as she giggled.

Giggled. A sound MacKenzie wouldn't have even thought the woman could make.

The day was getting worse by the second.

"Looks like we aren't the only ones feeling frisky," Josh murmured in her ear. She stepped away, unsure of whether she was more irritated about her best friend and Josh's annoying sister, or the way his breath on her skin made her pulse race.

"*We* are not feeling anything," she said, resuming her brisk pace to get to the table. Setting her coffee down solidly, she glared at Andrea, and then looked at Kevin.

"You can go now. You'll be gone the rest of the day, right?"

He shrugged, and then winked. At Andrea.

"I'll be back later, I think. See how things are going." Then he slipped out of the small space and into the store, leaving MacKenzie to watch that blush deepen one more shade.

Andrea watched him go. Looking at MacKenzie, she tried to look nonchalant.

"So...how long have you two known--"

MacKenzie held up a hand and shook her head. "No. We are not doing this. You want to know about Kevin, talk to Kevin. Right now, I think we should just all focus on work." She looked around frantically, relieved when she saw a family headed toward their table with three small children. "Look, we have customers."

The rest of the day was a blur as MacKenzie talked superheroes and anti-heroes and graphic novels with anyone who cared to listen. Traffic was steady for most of the day, though admittedly most people stopped for the food first, the comic books being a secondary diversion. When it was all over, she had to admit that Andrea's crew had done a great job of keeping the chocolate fountain sauce away from her end of the table, and when Andrea invited her to dip a treat or two before they cleaned up, she accepted.

Choosing an innocent-looking sugar cookie, she held it under the chocolate stream. As the sauce enveloped the cookie, someone jostled her from behind.

On a normal day, she would have bumped the table, caught herself with her free hand, and maybe got some extra sauce on the one holding the cookie.

But in her overtired, under-caffeinated state, her free hand missed the edge of the table. Her cookie hand sank deep under the chocolate stream, hitting the center of the fountain and sending it wobbling on the table. In a desperate attempt to keep it from falling, she wrapped her other hand around the back of the fountain.

Her feet slipped out from underneath her and she fell backwards, pulling the fountain with her as she hit the ground hard, her head saved only by the body of whoever had been standing right behind her.

In a rather surreal moment, she saw some of the sauce fly over her head before the rest of it hit her face and torso, coating her in a too-warm-for-comfort sugary bath. The fountain itself left a dent in her stomach before finally rolling off onto the floor.

* * * * *

Josh shifted, careful to hold MacKenzie's head until he could get his leg more solidly underneath it. A few inches to the right or left and she'd have hit the floor, probably cracking her skull. He was going to fire that caterer who'd squeezed between them, pushing her into the table.

"Kenzie? Are you okay? Say something?"

"She can't say anything, you idiot - she probably can't breathe," Andrea answered for her. "Someone get me a towel. Make that several towels."

One of the staff ran off, and reappeared with a stack of kitchen towels from the back. He handed several to Andrea, and then some to someone behind Josh.

Andrea knelt down and wiped the green goop off MacKenzie's face and hands. "Just hold still for a second," she told MacKenzie. "There. Can you open your eyes?"

Josh held his breath as Kenzie reached up with her semi-clean hands and gave her eyelids a final swipe before carefully opening them. Her eyes met Josh's, then moved to Andrea, and finally settled on a point past Josh's face, widening in a mixture of shock and horror.

Josh looked up to see Mr. Williams, the mall manager staring down at them. His face was streaked with green, and a big green splotch ran down the side of what appeared to be a rather expensive suit.

Perfect.

Josh looked back down at Kenzie and stroked the side of her face with one hand.

"Are you okay? Anything broken?"

She hesitated a moment - long enough to make Josh wonder if she had actually hit her head somehow.

"I don't know," she finally said. "Someone help me up." She started to move, and he put a hand on each of her shoulders, holding her in place.

"I don't think you should move," he said.

Andrea nodded. "You landed flat on your back. We'll call an ambulance. You need a doctor to check you out."

"Nonsense. I'm fine, just a little stunned. I didn't even hit my head, thanks to Josh." MacKenzie struggled, wiggling out of his grasp. The leftover chocolate coating her shirt didn't help his grip, and he was forced to let her go or risk pulling her down forcefully. She sat up and tested her joints, starting at her fingers and finishing at her ankles.

Josh got to his feet, casting a sidelong glance at the manager who stood watching, arms crossed over his chest.

"It was an accident," Josh remarked, bending down to lend a hand when he saw MacKenzie start to get up. "And you should still go to the hospital," he told her, noting the wince as she straightened, green chocolate dripping off her soaked shirt onto the floor. Under different circumstances, seeing her dipped in chocolate would have been the highlight of his day, but considering the broad audience, he refrained from sharing the thought.

"Yes, well, I think I remember Ms. Jones objecting to your use of this fountain. Is that true?"

Andrea glared at MacKenzie. "You told him that?"

Kenzie shook her head. "No, of course not." She turned to the manager. "How--"

Mr. Williams shook his head. "Not important. The important thing is, they used it against your wishes, and...well...this happened. You have every right to be angry. No one would blame you for...say...filing a formal complaint, even. It would be perfectly understandable, given the situation."

Josh rubbed his head with a hand. Clearly the manager wanted them gone, yesterday. He just had to figure out how to keep MacKenzie from getting tossed out with them. He started to say…something, he wasn't sure what, but MacKenzie beat him to it.

"Now wait a second. We negotiated. I agreed to let them use the fountain, and this was just an accident. There's no need to get all excited or make any rash decisions, and I won't be filing a complaint. And unless there are any customers left…" she looked around pointedly. "I don't think anyone else will be filing a complaint either, right?"

Mr. Williams sighed. "I trust you will be filing a workman's comp claim, at least?"

She hesitated, and Josh nodded for her, unwilling to let her sacrifice her health or her bank account just to sidestep the man's personal agenda.

"Yes, she will. And we'll make sure you get a copy of that, Mr. Williams. Now if you'll excuse us, my staff needs to clean up, and I'd like to get Ms. Jones to the hospital for a checkup. We can discuss this in more detail later, if you'd like?"

Williams looked from Josh to MacKenzie, to Andrea before offering a curt nod.

"Fine. Let's just save ourselves some trouble though, and discuss it at the next board meeting on Monday morning. I'm sure they'll be interested to hear all about your…negotiations." The leer he sent MacKenzie made Josh's blood boil, and he instinctively stepped in front of her. Williams raised an eyebrow and a small grin spread across his lips before he turned and walked away.

"We might as well just put the closed sign on the door and

start begging on the street," Andrea remarked, her arms folded over her chest. She shook her head, and turned to MacKenzie.

"Thank you, by the way. You tried, and we appreciate it." Her expression grew stern, and she glanced at Josh, and then back at MacKenzie, who looked like she was about to melt. "Now, you let Josh take you to the hospital, no arguments. And while you're driving, fix whatever it is that's making both of you crazy today. Whatever it is, it can't be that bad. So fix it."

"It is that bad," MacKenzie said, her voice quiet, tired. "But you're right, we need to address it. Just let me change into a clean t-shirt from the shop, and I'll be ready to go." She went into the store, her movements slow and deliberate, belying her insistence that she was fine. Josh started to go after her, but stopped when Kevin met her at the door, looked her over and then pulled her into a hug.

They spoke for a moment, and then Kevin looked up, meeting Josh's eye. He left MacKenzie long enough to come to the doorway.

"I've got this," he said, his tone brooking no argument. "She'll call you later." Without waiting for a response, he pulled the door closed and locked it, then put an arm around MacKenzie as they walked toward the back of the store.

"What's this about?" Andrea asked as Josh walked with her back into their store. "Why is she so upset?"

The last thing MacKenzie needed was Andrea jumping to the defense of their father, so Josh chose a believable lie instead.

"I think you were right, sis. Dating outside our social set just isn't going to work, and I need to move on, choose someone who's comfortable in our world."

She shook her head, a cynical laugh crossing her lips.

"Oh no. That girl," she pointed a thumb at the wall they shared with MacKenzie. "She can handle it. There has to be something else. What aren't you telling me?"

He held up both hands. "It's between me and MacKenzie. We'll either figure it out, or we won't. Just let it go. Let's get this place cleaned up, and get out of here."

He walked over to the table, surveying the damage. Thankfully most of the chocolate had gone off the table with MacKenzie, but a few of her books were still ruined. He set them aside, all too aware of Andrea's glare at his back while he packed up the rest of the comics into a box to be given back later.

He turned to return the glare, raising his eyebrows, but she held her ground.

"I'm not leaving until you tell me what's going on." She tapped her foot, blocking the path of the woman attempting to mop the floor around her.

He shrugged. "Fine. Then I'll leave. See you tomorrow." Brushing past her, he went through the store and out the back door, not even stopping for his coat. He'd go to the hospital and make sure MacKenzie was okay.

Then, in light of today's events, he had business to discuss with his dad.

* * * * *

"You sure you don't want to stop and get that prescription filled? There's a drug store just on the corner up ahead."

MacKenzie shook her head and then winced at the zinger the motion sent down her spine.

"Thanks Kev, but it's just a hyped up ibuprofen. I'll save the money and use what I've got at home. I really just need to crawl into bed and sleep it all off."

Kevin chuckled from the driver's seat beside her. "I hate to remind you, but it always hurts worse a couple days later. But sleep will help your mood, anyways." He gave her a sidelong glance as they sat at a red light. "So are you ready to tell me what's going on between you and Josh? He stopped by while you were getting checked out, by the way. I told him he should call you later."

MacKenzie sighed, willing away the flush that started in her face at the mere mention of his name. Thank goodness it was dark.

She wanted to see Josh, or her body did, at least. She wanted to feel his arms around her, hear him telling her it would be all right. That they'd figure something out about the mall, and everything else too.

But it didn't seem possible. "It turns out we have an...irreconcilable difference," she said finally as Kevin turned onto her street. "I just don't think there's any way to make it work."

He pulled the car into her driveway and shut off the engine, leaning forward to peer at something through the windshield. Raising a hand, he pointed toward her front porch.

"I wouldn't count him out just yet," Kevin said. She looked at where he was pointing, and a familiar figure sat on her front steps. Waiting.

"Want me to stay?" Kevin asked, leaning back in his seat. MacKenzie shook her head.

"No." She sighed. "I can handle it. He won't be here long." Turning back to Kevin, she smiled. "Thank you for everything, Kev. I really appreciate all this."

He smiled. "You're welcome. I'll pick you up for work

tomorrow, unless you call and tell me not to. Okay?"

"Okay." She opened the door and carefully slid out, muscles she didn't even know existed protesting after sitting just for the ride from the hospital. Kevin was right - tomorrow was really going to hurt. Although tonight wasn't looking especially pain-free either.

Josh stood as she closed the car door, and she braced herself, expecting him to rush over and offer to help. But he waited for her to come to him, and she was grateful. She didn't think she could handle him touching her, as much as she'd relish the feel of him. She needed distance if they were going to have a reasonable conversation.

"I wanted to make sure you were okay," he said as she drew near. "I was worried." He started to reach out, and then withdrew, clearly fighting his instincts to help. She looked at him for a long moment, and then nodded.

"I'm fine - or I will be." Grasping the handrail, she looked up the steps and prepared for the pain. "Come inside. We need to talk."

All too aware of him behind her, she ascended one step at a time, her knee and back screaming at her to stop. The doctor said she'd twisted some parts one way, and other parts the other as she fell, and the muscle strains would heal in time.

Not too long, she hoped silently as she finally opened the door and let herself in. She heard Josh enter as well, and the door clicked shut behind him. Leading the way down the hall, MacKenzie went straight to the living room and sank into the plush cushions of her couch with a grateful sigh.

Josh sat in a matching chair across from her and leaned forward, elbows propped on his knees.

"I went to see my father after Kevin sent me away."

MacKenzie raised her eyebrows. She wasn't sure what she'd been expecting, but it wasn't that. Had he suddenly come around to her way of thinking? A tiny glimmer of hope flared in her heart, though she was afraid to trust it.

"About what, exactly?"

He looked down at his clasped hands. "About finding a property to move the catering business into. And your shop as well, if you're interested. There's a small strip mall in arrears that he's about to take over--"

"So after I tell you that I don't approve of how your family business does...business, you seem to think that somehow, I'd be interested in actually doing business with them? Are you insane?"

He sat back, running a hand through his hair. "Look, I know it's not ideal, but I can't just let Andrea's dream get shut down because the mall manager doesn't like us. You can even vet the buildings, make sure all the paperwork is correct and accounted for - hell, even check with the tax office to make sure nothing gets screwed up. It's a good deal, MacKenzie, for both of us. But we can't do it alone. We need at least one other business to move in, two if we can get it."

She shook her head, a small laugh of disbelief escaping her lips.

"So he can put those checks in place when it suits him, but not when it comes down to a little thing like someone's home? Oh right. Business is more important than people. Excuse me for forgetting that important little detail."

Josh stood up to pace. "I don't run the company, MacKenzie. I don't have any say in how my father does business. All I know is that this is a chance to save our stores, and we can make sure it's done ethically. Isn't that enough for now?"

She shook her head again. "No. No it's not."

He stopped in front of her, hands on his hips as he gave her a frustrated glare.

"So you're going to do what Williams wants then? File a complaint and get us kicked out? Because it seems like that's the only way you'll get to keep your spot in the mall. Is that the plan then?"

MacKenzie closed her eyes and let her head fall back against the couch.

"No Josh, I'm not going to do that either. I'm not sure what I'm going to do, okay? But there has to be a way to figure this out. I'm just...not really thinking straight." She felt him sit down beside her, the warmth of his body radiating her way. It made her shiver, and she realized she was cold.

He sighed, and she opened her eyes to look at him. There was no arrogance, no anger, not even judgment in his expression. Just a weary frustration that she identified with all too well.

"I don't want to fight anymore," she said, looking away again. "Let's give it the night to sit, okay? Maybe once we're rested, the solution will come to us."

His fingers settled gently over her hand, and she knew she should pull away, but just couldn't. Gently rubbing, they slid between hers, giving a light squeeze. She closed her eyes again. Tired. So very tired.

"Okay," he said, his voice low and mellow. "Tomorrow. And MacKenzie?"

She hesitated before answering, trying to keep from dozing off. "Yes?"

"We need to find a way to make this work between us too. There has to be a way, right?"

"There's always a way," she murmured, shivering. "We'll figure it out."

She barely felt him extricating his fingers from hers, and warmth finally surrounded her as she drifted off to sleep.

* * * * *

MacKenzie woke with a solid wall of warmth at her back, and she shivered, wondering why the front of her was cold, save for a single band of heat wrapped around her middle. She shifted slightly and groaned as various muscles protested the movement, and the warm band tightened over her waist.

The pain brought her fully awake, and she blinked against the bright light coming in through the semi-transparent curtains that hung in her living room. Her head hurt, but then so did most everything else.

"Oh. My. God." She groaned again as she swung her legs off the couch and sat up, watching the sturdy, muscular arm slide off her hip, fingers flexing as if they were reluctant to let go.

Josh. Last night he'd sat beside her on the couch, and she'd closed her eyes for just a minute...

Long fingers stroked her sore back and she twisted to look behind her, wincing at the pain.

"You're still here," she said, facing forward again to alleviate the pain. "Why are you still here?" She rubbed her face with her hands, standing up to give him room as he started to move.

"I fell asleep." His feet touched the floor, and then one moved to rest on the other side of where she stood. His hands grasped her hips, pulling her backward. "You've got to be sore. Let me rub out the kinks."

She sat back on the couch between his legs, not awake enough yet to argue. It hurt, his fingers kneading her neck and shoulders, moving down to dig into the big knots on either side of her spine, but every time he moved to a new spot, the one he'd just left felt...passably good. She closed her eyes and tried to ignore how his touch was turning her on. How being this close to him was making her forget that she was mad. Or anything, really, aside from wanting to feel his lips at the nape of her neck. His fingers under her shirt, moving against her bare skin. His thighs tighter against hers.

She had to move. Now. Before she did something she'd really regret.

Maybe.

Summoning all her strength, she got off the couch and took a few steps away, out of reach.

"Um...thank you. That helped a lot, actually."

He looked confused, and a little irritated, but this was the right thing to do. For both of them.

Probably.

He looked like he was going to argue, and she didn't want to hear it. Not yet. Not before coffee, at the very least.

"I'm going to go shower." She pointed over her shoulder toward the hall. "There's a coffee maker in the kitchen, and everything's in the cupboard above that. Help yourself. I won't be long."

She turned and walked away, practically sprinting down the hall and locking herself in the bathroom. Flipping on the light, she came face to face with herself in the mirror.

"What the hell are you doing, Kenz?" She kept her voice low

and leaned closer to her rumpled reflection. "Do not fall for this guy. He's bad news. File the complaint and be done with it. With him."

Looking into her own eyes, she almost believed she could do it. Then she sighed, cringed at the tangled mane sticking out at odd angles and turned away from the mirror. Who was she kidding? She'd already fallen head-over-Keds for her very own anti-hero. What would Charade do?

Stepping under the shower spray, MacKenzie shook her head. Charade would do what any self-respecting hero would do - she'd take down the father's business, and then win back the son's heart because she was totally awesome like that.

Too bad MacKenzie wasn't Charade. And Josh was right - his father wasn't doing anything illegal. Which left her only two choices: agree to disagree about the family business and try to build a relationship in spite of it, or she had to cut this...whatever they were doing off now.

And mean it.

She spent a long time in the shower, getting out only when the water ran cold. She toweled off and wished she'd thought to grab clean clothes before shrugging into the fluffy robe she kept hanging on the back of the door. Hurrying across the hall to her room, she changed quickly and made her way back out to the kitchen, a little irked that she didn't smell hot coffee along the way, and a lot nervous to run into Josh again.

But the house was empty, and on the counter in front of her coffee pot, there was a note.

"There's something I need to do. See you at work. J"

MacKenzie was pretty sure it was a bad sign that the lack of coffee was more annoying than the fact that he'd left without saying goodbye.

Setting up the coffee pot and turning it on, she stood by the counter and waited for the magic elixir to brew. The Charade scenario kept running through her mind, and there was something teasing at the edge of her mind...an answer, maybe, but she couldn't quite grasp it. When the coffee finished brewing, she filled her travel mug and screwed the lid on. Grabbing her purse and keys, she went out the door, completely forgetting that her car was still at the mall until she stood in her empty garage. Luckily, Kevin pulled into the driveway just then, and she tried to look like she wasn't surprised to see him at all.

They were halfway to work when the solution hit her. She couldn't touch Josh's father, of course, but she might be able to solve the real estate problem and keep his father's firm from making any money on it. It would be tight, but worth it, both for Kenzie's Comics and Taste the World.

It was a start.

"There's something I need to do," she told Kevin when he pulled into the mall parking lot. "Can you hold down the fort until I get back?"

He nodded. "Sure. Whatever you need, just take your time." The curiosity was plain on his face, but he didn't ask, and she didn't offer anything more. It was a long-shot, but she had to try. She changed cars and drove downtown, hoping her accountant was in.

Chapter 8

Josh parked behind the mall and entered the back of the catering shop, stopping long enough to locate Andrea in the kitchen. Moving carefully through the bustling staff, he went to her side.

"We need to talk," he said as she scooped some sort of filling into a dough cup of some sort.

She shook her head, not even sparing him a look. "Unless you want to talk here, you're going to have to wait, brother-dear. We're running late with this order and it's got to go out the door in two hours."

He looked around the stainless steel kitchen, noting the concentration on every single face. No one was paying particular attention, but this wasn't the sort of thing anyone else should hear.

"Two hours then. Come to my office when you're done?"

"Yes boss," she teased, giving him a small grin before turning back to her work. "I promise your love-life won't evaporate before I get there."

"It's already gone," he replied, walking away before she could quiz him further. Time enough for that after they'd made some decisions.

At his desk he opened up the bookkeeping program and ran

down the financials for the last two months again. It would be tight, but with what he had in savings, and what he thought Andrea had, they should have just enough to make a non-offensive bid for that strip mall his father wanted to foreclose on.

If they could buy it outright, MacKenzie wouldn't be able to object at how it was obtained, and maybe he could talk her into moving the comic shop.

As a bonus, they'd own the building, so they wouldn't have to worry about being kicked out. Just making the monthly payments.

He checked his watch. Only half an hour had passed, and he couldn't do anything unless Andrea agreed. He opened a few more files, did a little more paperwork, checked his watch again.

A whole hour left to go.

Pushing back from his desk, he walked down to the coffee stand, ignoring Kenzie's Comics as he passed by the first time. On his way back, the door was open and he couldn't resist a little peek. Trevor was behind the counter, reading a comic book.

He considered going inside and telling MacKenzie his plan, but something told him to wait, so he went back to his desk.

Forty minutes to wait.

Unable to just sit, he called his father's office and got the information he needed to contact the company that owned the strip mall. The foreclosure wasn't scheduled for a couple of days yet, so it couldn't hurt to feel them out a bit, see what kind of offer they might be willing to accept. Stuck on hold for the next twenty minutes, he finally gave up when Andrea walked in the door.

"Five minutes early," she said, grinning as she collapsed in a chair. "So what did you want to talk about?"

He braced his elbows on the desk and leaned forward.

"Do you still have your part of the money we inherited from Wallace?"

Andrea frowned. "Some of it - I put most of it into this place. Why?"

He sat back in his chair. "If you have two million, I have five, and we've got a couple to play around with from this place. I think we should put an offer on that strip mall I told you about - buy it outright, instead of leasing from Dad."

Andrea sighed. "So MacKenzie turned you down? I don't see why we can't just find two other stores to join us. I know you're in love with the girl, but you're talking about a lot of money. Did she give a reason?"

Josh hesitated, not sure how much he should reveal.

"She...has reservations with the way our father does business. So she's not comfortable leasing from him."

Audrey nodded, her eyes lighting with understanding.

"So that's what you two have been fighting about. And now you want to empty out our savings accounts just to accommodate this woman? That seems more like an emotional decision than a professional one to me."

Josh shrugged. "I'll admit it's partially emotional. And maybe not the best use of our savings, considering we could use the property cheaper if we just let Dad's company repossess it."

"Then why bother? Why not hold on to our money, let MacKenzie do what she wants, and just take care of ourselves?"

"Because we aren't making money fast enough," Josh said, looking her straight in the eye. "The catering business is slow growth right now - and while that may not always be the case, we could use the second income from strip mall rents to carry us through until the catering business is more solvent. It's a good location for MacKenzie too, so I'm sure if we got her in, she'd stay. Having at least one other occupant when we take possession will look better that having none."

Andrea shook her head. "Until she decides she really can't handle the relationship between you too. And then she's gone, and we're out a tenant. It's just a really bad idea, Josh. I'm sorry. I can't risk my savings on an emotional whim. I won't."

The phone in Andrea's office started to ring. "I have to get that." She got up and jogged next door, where Josh heard her pick up the phone, say a few words, and put it back down. She was standing in his doorway two seconds later.

"Mr. Williams is on his way back. He wants to talk to us."

* * * * *

It was afternoon before MacKenzie finally got to work. Kevin had already left for the day, and Trevor tapped his watch and gave her a disapproving look.

"I'm gonna be late for class, Kenzie - you promised that wouldn't be a problem."

She nodded, waving him off. "I know, I'm sorry. Something important came up. It won't happen again. Go."

He looked like he wanted to argue, but after one more glance at his watch he slung his backpack over one shoulder and jogged out the back door. Kenzie listened to the door slam, put the bell on the front counter and went back to the workroom to stow her keys and get a cup of coffee from a pot that had undoubtedly been sitting for most of the day.

Back at the front counter, she sat on the hard, high stool and reflected on what she'd just done.

She'd made an offer on, and provisionally bought, the strip mall Josh's dad would have foreclosed on.

Her accountant had tried to talk her out of it, but when she refused to budge, he'd ultimately found a way for her to finance part of the new venture. It hinged on the profitability of Kenzie's Comics for the next several years though, and in smaller part on Taste the World. Along with several other tenants she'd need to find and cultivate.

She'd toured the building, checked out the location, and gone over all the financials for the past three years, plus building codes and inspection reports. Her head was still spinning with all the figures, but the owner had been desperate to get it all done quickly, as if she might vanish into thin air if they let her think about it too long.

Which, in hindsight was probably a bad sign. But she'd ignored that, focusing instead on what could be. She'd signed a provisional contract just an hour before, that gave her a week before the formal closing to reconsider her purchase.

The enormity of it all was just starting to sink in, and as she went through the motions of helping customers, restocking inventory and updating the books, the weight of all the extra responsibilities settled down on her shoulders. Thinking it would help, she made lists of what she'd need to get done, both for the comic shop and for the strip mall.

It only made her more depressed. There was no way she could do it on her own. She needed help.

* * * * *

MacKenzie had just locked the front doors and settled into her office chair, staring at the provisional agreement again when there was a knock at the back door. She went to open it, expecting Kevin or Trevor and hopeful that she'd finally have someone to talk her out of the rash decision she'd made.

But it was Josh on the other side, with a serious expression she imagined mirrored her own. She opened the door wide, closing it after he stepped into the storage room.

"You look like hell," she said, gesturing for him to take a seat at the long table in the middle of the room. "Wanna talk about it?"

He shook his head at first, and he looked so dejected that she walked over and put a hand on his shoulder, squeezing gently in support. He reached up to cover it with his own, just holding on for a moment before he tugged her around to face him.

"The mall is evicting us," he said quietly. "Apparently they can't throw us out just because they don't like Andrea, but our revenues aren't what we projected when we signed the contract, and that's enough to cancel it."

She nodded sympathetically. Now would probably be a good time to share her news. Maybe he'd help her with the mall. It couldn't hurt to ask. "Well, you knew they were looking for a way to toss you out. And that strip mall--"

He shook his head again, looking down at his lap. "Someone bought it. Today, I guess, before the foreclosure could be finalized. I was going to make an offer myself, but Andrea won't help, and I just don't have enough on my own."

"Josh, listen to me." He looked up at her, and the sheer hopelessness in his eyes nearly made her cry. Except she could fix it. Or she thought she could.

"I bought the strip mall. This morning. It's going to be a lot of work, but if you'll help me, I think we can--"

Josh sat back in his chair, shock lining his face.

"You bought that mall? This morning? By yourself? Are you crazy?"

MacKenzie frowned. "I was just trying to convince myself I wasn't crazy, actually. I thought you'd be happy. I thought us moving our stores into the mall together was what you wanted..."

Getting up from the table, Josh paced the length of the room. "I did. I do. But I just assumed that I...that my father..." He didn't finish his sentence, but it wasn't all that hard to figure out what he was trying to say.

"You thought it was a good idea when your father would own it, or if you bought it yourself. What's the matter, Josh? Scared to have me as your landlord? Worried I won't treat you fairly?"

"I don't know," he said, his tone tired and frustrated. "I just thought it would be a way Andrea and I could finally have some security, and I'm just not sure how that can be if we don't have any ownership rights. It's nothing against you personally, Kenzie. But this morning I wanted to buy that place, and Andrea told me it was for the wrong reasons. Now that you've gone ahead and bought it and...I don't know how to feel."

MacKenzie nodded, considering his words. If he was being honest, then he should have no problem with her proposal. If not, and it was her he objected to...well, there was still time to back out of the sale, thank goodness.

Getting up, she stood in his path, placing both hands lightly against his chest.

"Okay then - how about this? I can't run both the comic shop and the mall by myself. Buy in for whatever you can afford, and we'll manage the strip mall together."

* * * * *

Her touch made his brain take a while longer than normal to process her words, but when Josh realized what she was offering, he met her eyes and really looked at her for the first time since he'd walked in.

Shadowed in the fatigue and worry was a spark of hope, but he wasn't sure what it was for, exactly. Andrea's lecture poked at him, forced him to clarify, for both their sakes.

"You're offering joint ownership and management of the mall? If you already signed the papers, getting a new contract drawn up could be expensive and tricky..."

She shrugged. "I have a week to withdraw from the contract. The owner is so desperate to sell that I'm sure if we go talk to him and tell him what we want to do, he'll void my contract, and we can have a new one written up. You can have whatever percentage you like up to fifty. Everything in writing and legally binding. If one of us wants out, the other can buy the half in question, or we liquidate. Fair enough?"

Josh moved away - he needed to think, and her touching him wasn't working. He considered her proposal and couldn't think of any issues, except one.

"Why are you doing this, Kenzie? You're not being evicted, your business is doing well here, and the mall might even give you a more suitable neighbor once we're gone. Why leave?"

She leaned against the table, arms crossed over her chest.

"Mostly for the security," she said, not even taking time to think. "If I own the building, or even part of it, I don't have to worry about losing my store to the whims of someone deciding they don't like me for whatever reason."

He nodded, moving to stand in front of her, forcing her to look up at him. "Mostly? What's the other reason?"

"A point of compromise," she said, holding his stare with her own. "We said we'd try to work it out - this thing between us, I mean. If we work together on this, your dad's out of the picture, our stores both have a good chance of success, and you and I...can work on things too."

Josh heard Andrea's voice in his head, berating him for letting emotions have any place in a business decision. And she was right, dammit.

It did seem like the perfect plan, as far as the stores and contracts went. The emotional part was trickier, and if he and MacKenzie couldn't make it work, they'd lose everything. He knew for a fact Andrea would think the risk was too high.

There was only one way this could work. He could either have one, or the other. Not both.

And he hated it.

Cupping her jaw, he relished the surprise and anticipation in Kenzie's eyes as he bent down to place a soft, slow kiss on her lips. When he pulled back, she made to follow him, but he stepped out of reach.

"Kenzie, I think we have to let this thing - this relationship," he pointed to her, and then back to himself. "Go. It's too risky to sign a contract we're destined to break if we can't figure out how to get along, and given how you feel about my father, I think we need to choose - either the partnership, or the relationship. I'm sorry, but we just can't do both. I can't do both."

* * * * *

MacKenzie rubbed her forehead with one hand, and then crossed her arms over her chest again. She hadn't seen that coming, but Josh was right. The contract essentially locked them together, and if something went south with the relationship and one of them couldn't afford the buyout price, they'd both lose everything, both personally and professionally.

It wasn't fair to put themselves in that position, no matter how convenient it might be. Then again, working closely together could only be a step in the right direction, and maybe later, when they were both settled and the businesses were solvent...well, you never knew.

She pushed away from the table and went to stand in front of him, holding out her right hand.

"Business partners, then," she said, forcing a cool, professional smile to her face. "Let's get our houses in order, so to speak. After that, who knows?"

He held her stare for a long moment, and then nodded, a glimmer of hope in his eyes for the first time since he'd come in. His handshake was firm as she knew it would be, and a sense of peace settled alongside the resignation she felt. Maybe things couldn't work out between them right now...but they'd be working closely together, and even though the focus would be on the business, there was at least a chance for friendship.

"Let me just call my lawyer, and the mall owner so we can get new papers drawn up. If you want to call yours..." She went to her desk and picked up the phone, happy to see that Josh already had his out.

"On it," he said, putting the phone to his ear. He flashed her a quick smile before turning away to talk, and she knew that somehow, someday, this was all going to work out as it should.

97

Chapter 9

Three months later...

The sun was sinking fast when MacKenzie locked the front door of the comic shop and then went through the back into a narrow hallway that spanned the length of the strip mall. She was headed to the main business office at the end of the building, where she planned to spend another couple of hours doing paperwork, as she had been ever since the sale of the mall was finalized and she and Josh had moved their stores in. They'd tried working at the same time but it had proved too distracting for both of them to be in the small space at once, so by silent agreement she stayed at night, and he put in a few hours early in the morning. A secretary answered calls for them during the day, taking messages and re-routing calls to either Kenzie or Josh's cell phones when necessary.

Everything had been working out well so far, she thought with a smile as she let herself into the office. Both stores were turning a profit, foot traffic was up, and with the addition of two more stores and one moving in starting tomorrow, revenue was increasing quickly. By this time next year, she anticipated having a healthy emergency fund set aside for the business, and being able to give both herself and Josh a raise on the administration side.

Just the thought of him still made her skin flush, and she shook her head at the automatic response. Passing his cubicle in the corner, she breathed in deeply to inhale his lingering scent, and then castigated herself for the girlish gesture. Aside from the occasional sighting coming or going, she hadn't seen him much in the last couple of months and when she did, they were always careful to be polite and businesslike - nothing more, nothing less. For all she knew he'd moved on, and nothing was stopping her from doing the same.

This was working. Business was good. Life was uncomplicated. Everything was the way it was supposed to be.

Wasn't it?

Settling in at her desk she logged into her computer and opened up the bookkeeping program. When the phone rang twenty minutes later, the sound made her jump in her chair.

"Cedar Strip Mall," she said, not recognizing the number on the caller ID.

"Hey," a rich, rather yummy-sounding male voice said in her ear. "This is Matt Avery - the Bike Shop owner. I was hoping to catch someone in the office - I couldn't make it down earlier, and I was wondering if I could pick up my keys so we could start moving stuff in tomorrow."

The man sounded...manly. And in good shape. She wondered if he had that sexy five-o-clock shadow that the rough and tumble types made look so good. And strong, biker-shaped thighs. Her cheeks warmed, and she nearly laughed out loud at herself putting together a drool-worthy athlete based only on the sound of his voice. Josh had been the one to meet with him and sign the contracts, but Kenzie had been looking forward to meeting their newest tenant.

Seemed like now she'd get her chance.

"Hello? Are you there?"

She rolled her eyes at herself. "I'm here - sorry. And if you want to meet me out front, I'd be happy to give you your keys. How far away are you?"

"I'm actually in the parking lot now."

"Great! Be out in a minute."

Kenzie hung up the phone and went to Josh's cube, finding the keys tacked neatly to one of the fabric-covered walls with a note that said "Avery". Hesitating for a moment, she took the keys and let herself into the back hallway again, finding her way to the door marked 212 and opening it to walk through the empty space to the front of the store.

A man waited on the sidewalk just outside, hands tucked loosely into his worn jeans and a jersey of some sort left hanging in the breeze. Clean-shaven, he did look like he was in good shape, and when she pushed the door open from the inside, he smiled, pinning her with a gorgeous pair of baby blues.

She smiled back, silently reminding herself not to drool over the new tenant as she extended her hand.

"You must be Matt. I'm MacKenzie. It's nice to meet you."

* * * * *

The next morning Josh unlocked the main office and sat down at his desk to find a note in MacKenzie's handwriting on his desk. He made a point to ignore the quickening of his pulse at the sight. Scanning it, he glanced up to note that Avery's keys were indeed gone, though she'd left the note and tack in the wall.

He wished she'd told him in person, though he understood why she'd left a note instead. But would it always be this way? Would there ever come a time when they could be in the same room together and not feel awkward just talking like normal people?

Would he ever not want her?

Tossing the note in the trash, he turned to his computer. He'd been the one to insist on this professional wall between them, and as much as he'd like to say the hell with it and burn it down, it seemed like a bad idea so early in their partnership.

Or that's what he told himself when he got the urge to stalk down the hall and drag her into his arms for the kiss he imagined would put their partnership squarely at the mercy of their emotions.

Bad business.

Tuning out the nagging voice in the back of his head insisting he go all caveman on his favorite comic shop girl, he opened a few files and got to work. Forty minutes later he closed them again, unable to focus on anything but seeing MacKenzie again.

Maybe he'd just take the outside route to the catering shop this morning, check on Avery as he went by. Maybe wave at MacKenzie if she happened to be in this early, though that was highly unlikely...

It was a beautiful morning - sunny, bright and cool. There was a big truck backed into the space directly in front of the new bike shop, and several athletic-looking guys unloading what looked like racks and shelving as he approached. Matt Avery smiled when he walked up, holding out his hand.

"Gorgeous day, isn't it? Makes me wish I was out riding instead of working, but I'm really happy with the space. Thanks again for letting us join you."

Josh grinned. "It's our pleasure, I assure you. We're just glad to see the place filling up. Any problems so far? I see you got the keys from Kenzie last night."

Avery shook his head with a sideways glance at his workers. "No problems at all. And MacKenzie seems nice. We talked for a bit when I got the keys." He started to say something else, then stopped, giving Josh an appraising look. "Do you know if she's seeing anyone, by any chance?"

Josh fought to stay calm and not give himself away.

"Um...I really don't know. You'd have to ask her. Sorry I can't help."

Matt nodded, looking down for a moment. "That's cool, man. I just thought maybe...well, the way she talks about you, I just wondered if you two were--"

More than anything Josh wanted to confirm those suspicions, but he couldn't. She deserved whatever chances came her way, and given her feelings about his family, Avery might be the better option.

She deserved to be happy.

"No." Josh shook his head. "We're not together, but thanks for checking." He looked at his watch. "Hey listen, I've got to run meet Andrea at the shop, but I'll see you later. Let me or MacKenzie know if you need anything, okay?"

Avery grinned. "You bet. Thanks again, man." He disappeared back inside the shop and Josh walked around the truck and down the sidewalk, making a point not to look in the shop window as he approached Kenzie's Comics. Watching the sidewalk instead, he frowned when he walked through a puddle of water just outside her front door nearly an inch deep.

It hadn't rained for days.

The water was flowing toward the parking lot, and he did look in the still-dark windows then, cupping his hands around his face for a better view. His heart sank when he saw the entire floor of her shop was now a shimmering, shallow lake.

* * * * *

MacKenzie's eyes narrowed as she pulled into her parking spot behind the strip mall. The back door near her shop was propped open, and a man in what looked like hip waders came out, tossed a bucket of dirty water towards the nearby drain and went back inside.

Kenzie turned off the engine and got out of the car, watching as another guy repeated the previous actions, and then went back inside. Panic rolled her stomach as she jogged toward the door, barely missing a third man coming out to dump a bucket of water.

"What's going on?" she asked as she followed him back inside. A small logo on the side of his plastic pants sported the name of a restoration company she didn't recognize. A lump formed in her throat.

"One of the old water pipes burst," he said, his tone gruff. "A couple of shops got pretty w--"

A strong hand grabbed Kenzie's arm and kept her from following the man into her store. Off balance, she had no choice but to let the momentum twirl her around and she stumbled, falling against a tall, firm, all-too-familiar body.

As quick as she made contact, he held her away, supporting her with a hand on each arm until she was steady.

"Don't go in there yet," Josh said, his eyes confirming her

worst fears. "One of the pipes between our stores...an older fitting came loose and it was right between our two shops."

She stepped back and looked at the floor, trying to process exactly what he meant. The shiny concrete underfoot only served to make the problem more real. She spun on her heel and strode toward the comic store, needing to see the damage herself.

"Kenzie, no. Wait!"

Ignoring Josh's plea, she side-stepped one of the cleanup crew and into the back office of the store. There was probably an inch of water still covering the floor, and the line on the walls suggested it had been higher. Which meant all the computer equipment sitting on the floor would have to be replaced. She noted it had all been unplugged.

The door had been closed last night, and even though she knew it was futile she found herself hoping the major damage had been contained here. Moving through and into the back hall, she turned left and looked into the store room. The lump in her throat grew more constrictive as she took in the boxes on the floor, soggy and sagging, full of inventory waiting to be cataloged and stocked. Several stacks of comic books had also met their end, and the sight of several floating loose on top of the lake brought tears to her eyes.

"You don't have to do this," Josh said from behind her, his hands caressing her shoulders. "Wait until they get the water cleaned up, and then assess the damages."

She shook her head, dashing a hand across her face to wipe away stray tears as she pulled out of his grasp.

"It's my store. I have to see. I have to know." Brushing past him she went out to the main showroom and stopped short, restoration men moving efficiently around her as she tried to take it all in. The path of the water was painfully obvious in the destruction left behind. To her left, it looked like a giant upside-down fan had crashed against the wall under a broken valve, leaving a crumpled mass of brilliant reds, yellows, blues and greens co-mingling the shelves in its wake.

Torn pages, ripped covers, and brightly colored bits were stuck in random patterns on at least half of the exposed flat surfaces, as well as swirling in the water being mopped up even as she watched. The entire store smelled musty, shirts hung in the flood and acted like wicks, water lapped against the shelves on the other side of the room, bathing expensive action figures and game pieces as it sloshed with every booted step and swirl of a mop. The front door stood propped open and more men were pushing water out the front door with long squeegees, making even more waves.

Kenzie couldn't move. Couldn't speak. She wasn't even sure what to think as she stood there watching her dreams just...melt.

Comforting hands came around her from behind, and she didn't fight when Josh picked her up and cradled her against his chest, carrying her away from it all.

* * * * *

MacKenzie barely suppressed a pathetic whimper when Josh put her down on the couch in the main office. For the few minutes he'd carried her, she hadn't felt quite so alone, and when he pulled away, the loneliness slid back in to take his place. He knelt at her feet, his hands working quickly to remove her soaked shoes and socks, squeezing the water out of her pant legs as well as he could.

"This is just a setback," he said, his voice calm and soothing. "We'll get everything cleaned up, and take the opportunity to do a little remodeling. It'll be better than ever." He smiled, the expression so warm and hopeful. And just like that, all the old feelings came rushing back, and she wanted to fling herself into his arms and kiss him senseless just for trying to make her feel better.

She didn't, of course. Couldn't. And she needed some space, now, before she made any more of a fool of herself than she already had clinging to him like a child.

Wiping the tears from her face she pulled her legs up on the couch and out of his reach. Taking a deep breath and letting it out again, she forced a small cool smile.

"You're right, it'll be fine. I'm just really tired, is all and that was...a shock. Would you mind keeping an eye on everything while I make a few calls? I should let Kevin and Trevor know before they come in."

His own smile faded, and she knew he felt it, the detachment she was trying to reestablish between them. If she didn't know better she'd almost think he was disappointed, but that was probably just her projecting her own wishes on him.

He took a step back, respecting the invisible wall. It literally hurt her heart to feel the gap between them widen.

"Sure. I need to check on Andrea's shop too. Let me know if you need anything."

She nodded, watching him walk away. She wanted to call him back, to thank him for taking care of everything, including her. To recapture that feeling of togetherness that seemed so effortless when they weren't actively trying to block it.

Letting her head fall back to rest against the back of the couch, she closed her eyes, wondering if they'd ever be able to be in the same room without fighting their attraction.

Or if she'd ever feel that connection with anyone else.

She heard the door open again, and opened her eyes in time to see Josh coming toward her with a serious, almost angry look on his face and a purpose-driven stride. She put her feet on the ground and stood as he drew closer.

"What's wrong? Did something else happen?"

He stopped too close for comfort, but when she went to move back, he reached out and pulled her close, bending to capture her lips in a searing kiss that left her raw, wanting and completely at his mercy.

Chapter 10

Josh groaned as Kenzie melted against him, pulling her closer as he gentled the pressure against her lips. After months of restraint, the energy built up between them was enough to make him want to lay her down and ravage her right there on the couch, but somehow he managed to let her go when she pushed against his chest.

Confusion and uncertainty pooled in her eyes as she stepped back out of reach and folded her arms over her chest. He reached for her, wanting her close, but she shook her head.

"Josh, we should…talk, don't you think?"

He shook his head. Talking just seemed to force them farther apart. He didn't want to think, and based on how she'd responded to his kiss, she didn't really either.

"No." He shook his head. "I think we work better when we don't talk, actually. Come here."

Her eyes widened, and she took a step back, but he saw the look of desire that crossed her face before she neutralized it. She wanted him. He wanted her more than anything, and he was convinced that if they just went with the chemistry they could make everything else work. Somehow.

He took a step forward, one hand held out to her. "Aren't you tired of fighting it? God, MacKenzie. I can't think when you're within twenty feet of me, and you're all I can think about for hours after I've seen you, even if it's just for a few seconds. You're in my blood, and I know it's not just me feeling this way. Can't we just...quit fighting? See what happens?"

She looked away, shaking her head. "I can't. I need more. I need to know this isn't just about sex, or attraction, or our damn hormones. There are so many things we don't agree on, and just following the chemistry isn't going to change that--"

"One." Josh stalked over to stand in front of her, not touching her, just glaring down into her eyes. "There's one major thing we don't see eye-to-eye on, and I'll be straight with you Kenzie, we might never agree on my father's business. And that's okay, because people don't have to agree on everything to be good together. Then again, we might just figure out how to work it out. But we won't know unless we try, and denying the connection between us until then is just...stupid."

She gasped, her eyes narrowed and her face flushed red.

"You did not just call me stupid for wanting to think about this before we--"

"No!" He looked at the ceiling and grabbed his hair with his hands, frustration and adrenaline flooding his body in equal measure. When he looked back at her, she raised an eyebrow.

"I'm saying I don't want to be apart anymore. I was stupid to even think we could. We should be together. Call it fate, or kismet, or destiny, or whatever your comic book heroes would call it, but you know it's true, Kenzie." He sighed, lowering his voice. "I don't want to fight this anymore. I want...I need to be with you. Please."

* * * * *

"MacKenzie? Are you in here?"

Kenzie looked past Josh as Kevin came through the office door and spotted her. He jogged over, his expression a mixture of concern and frustration.

"What the hell happened to the store? Is everyone okay? There's water everywhere..." he glanced down at her bare feet and rolled up jeans. "Are you hurt?"

She shook her head, more relieved than she cared to admit that he'd shown up when he did.

"I'm fine, just a little soggy. One of the water pipes burst, and the comic shop and Andrea's kitchen got the worst of it."

Josh put his hands on his hips and turned away slightly, as if undecided about what to do next. Kevin glanced at him, and then back at her, eyebrows raised.

"You guys need a minute? Andrea's looking for Josh, but I can tell her--"

Josh shook his head. "It's okay. I'll go." He looked Kenzie in the eye and his frustration practically screamed at her to stop him, to give him the words he needed. They needed.

Instead, she just nodded, watching him walk away for the second time that morning and knowing that this time, he wouldn't be back. He'd told her how he felt, and now the ball was in her court, so to speak. If she wanted him, she'd have to tell him.

"So." Kevin pulled her attention back to him. "You guys finally going to hook up, or what?"

She shrugged, rubbed her hands over her face and sat back down on the couch, letting out a long sigh.

"I don't know. He wants to, I want to, but I just don't know if I can deal with...what we disagree on. It's confusing, and then there's the store and getting the mess cleaned up and the loss of income while we remodel..."

Kevin sat beside her and put an arm around her shoulders, pulling her in for a friendly hug.

"When it rains it pours - literally, it seems. But we'll deal with the store, Kenz. It happens, and you just pick up and keep moving forward. Charade is doing well so we have that as backup income, you have the mall, and everything will be okay."

She nodded, knowing he was right, even though it felt like her whole world was crumbling at the moment.

"As for Josh," Kevin said, "If you want my opinion, you're over thinking it. I don't know what your issues with him are, but the chemistry between you two is enough to burn down this building. Give it a chance. See where it goes. Even if it doesn't work, I think you'll regret not at least giving it a shot."

She pulled away so she could smile at him. "As much as I hate to admit it, I think you're right." She poked him lightly in the ribs. "Since when did you become a psychologist, anyways?"

He grinned back. "Since we started exploring Charade's dark and anti-hero-worthy past. Obviously I'm not doing a very good job if you've failed to learn anything while illustrating her story."

She rolled her eyes. "Yeah, yeah. My job is to make her look bad-ass even when she's going through the touchy-feely stuff, remember?"

Kevin laughed, extricating himself from the couch and holding out a hand to help her up.

"And you do a fine job too. Now let me start making some calls...I'll get in touch with the insurance company and see what we need to file the claim. You go find that broody guy of yours and settle things so you can both focus on wringing this place out, okay?"

She cocked her head to the side, thinking. "Maybe I should wait--"

"No." Kevin pointed to the door. "Go. Now. Neither of you can work effectively like this. Don't come back alone."

MacKenzie finally laughed, feeling like a heavy weight had been lifted off her shoulders.

"Okay! I'm going!" She forced herself to move at a casual walk until she got through the door. Then she jogged down the hall, careful not to slip on the damp floors with her bare feet.

Then a door opened, and there was no time to stop...

* * * * *

When she came to, MacKenzie was flat on her back, the dim florescent lights from the ceiling partially blocked by Matt-the-bike-shop-owner's head.

"Oh god, are you okay? I can't believe I hit you with the door. How's your head?"

Now that he mentioned it, her head felt like someone had bashed her skull in with a baseball bat. She groaned and moved to get up, stopped by strong hands holding her shoulders down.

"I don't think you should move," he said, looking away for a moment. "You probably have a concussion or something. Let me call Josh. Or 9-1-1."

"No, it's okay. I'm fine." MacKenzie rolled to the side, brushing his hands away as she fought a wave of nausea. Making it to her knees, she stopped, feeling the back of her head with one hand for a depression or bleeding.

"See any blood?" she asked, probing gingerly with her fingers. Matt moved her fingers aside and felt around the wound with his own before moving to face her.

"No, but you're going to have quite the bump." He stared into her eyes. "I really think you might have a concussion. You should get checked out. I can drive you to the hospital if you want..."

Footsteps came running down the hall and in two seconds Kevin was kneeling beside her, lips set in a thin line as he caressed the side of her face.

"What the hell happened? Are you hurt?"

"She ran into the door when I opened it," Matt said. "Hit her head pretty hard. I was just trying to convince her to go to the hospital."

Kevin took her hands and helped her up, supporting her when she had a hard time keeping her balance.

"Let's go - I'll drive. You need to see a doctor. No arguments."

MacKenzie shook her head, immediately regretting the movement.

"But I need to see Josh. Just take me--"

Kevin shook his head, and something in his expression made her stomach flip again. Or maybe that was the headache.

"He's not here, Kenzie. That's why I was coming to find you. His dad had a heart attack, and he and Andrea went to the hospital. They're not sure he's going to make it. Josh wanted you to know. He...wanted to know if you'd meet him there."

"Okay then." MacKenzie took a deep breath and fought back another wave of nausea. "I guess I'm going to the hospital, one way or the other. Matt, would you mind keeping an eye on things here until Kevin gets back? I know it's not your job, but since Josh and I are both out..."

Matt nodded. "No problem at all. Don't worry about anything, just take care."

MacKenzie let Kevin help her out to his car and winced as she got in the passenger seat and buckled her seatbelt. It was hard to stay awake on the quick drive to the hospital, and Kevin's incessant chatter was annoying, but he seemed insistent that she couldn't nap. And when the car finally stopped, she didn't understand why there was a nurse with a wheelchair waiting at the curb for them. Or why no one listened when she kept asking to see Josh...

* * * * *

Josh paced the too-shiny white hospital floor, waiting for any news of his father. Andrea sat with their mother across the room, but he couldn't stay still, though he knew the constant motion wasn't helping anyone relax. But his father was on the operating table, possibly dying. Relaxing didn't seem...right.

The big clock on the wall ticked down the seconds, an ominous sound even with the hustle and bustle of nurses and other assorted personnel swirling about. They'd been waiting nearly half an hour, and while he appreciated that open-heart surgery would require several, he didn't understand why the one person he wanted by his side still wasn't there.

He'd asked Kevin to find her. Been so sure she'd rush to his side. Selfish as it was, he wanted her there. Somehow he knew that if she was with him, everything would be okay. And after that kiss this morning...

Footsteps echoed down the corridor and he stopped pacing, hoping to see either the doctor or Kenzie come around the corner. When Kevin came into view instead, Josh felt something inside of him break.

She wasn't coming.

"It's not what you think," Kevin said, shaking his head for emphasis as he reached Josh. He was out of breath, as if he'd been running.

"Where is she? You said she'd come. I need her." Josh knew he'd spoken too loudly when heads turned toward him at his words, one nurse shaking her head, and a gasp coming from his mother's vicinity. He didn't care. "Where's Kenzie?"

Kevin shook his head again. "She was looking for you back at the mall. Fell and hit her head. She's here, but she's got a concussion. She's..." he hesitated, glancing in Andrea's direction before lowering his own voice to a murmur. "She's asking for you. I know you need to stay here, so I'll go sit with her until you're free. Just come find us when your dad's out of the woods. Room 212."

Kevin squeezed his arm, a gesture Josh assumed was supposed to be comforting before the man turned and went back the way he came. Josh watched him go, torn between his duty to stay and be with his family, and his need to make sure Kenzie - his soul mate - would be okay. He didn't move, just stood frozen in an indecisive angst.

A hand curved over one of his forearms and he twitched, startled at the touch. Andrea stood beside him, her eyes glassy and her face lined with concern.

"I asked the nurse," she said, gently rubbing his arm. "It's going to be another hour before we hear anything about Dad. Go. Make sure Kenzie's okay. I'll call if there's any change."

Josh shook his head. "She'll be okay. It's just a concussion. Kevin's with her. I should be here."

"You are here," Andrea said, giving him a slight smile. "And you can't do anything for Dad except wait. Go. See MacKenzie. You can help her - she needs you."

Pulling her into his arms, Josh gave his sister a big hug.

"Room 212. Call if there's any change at all, and I'll be back in a flash."

She nodded and he hesitated just one more minute, and then jogged toward the elevators.

Chapter 11

MacKenzie was relieved when Kevin finally came back into the tiny room they'd put her in, and she thought the doctor looked relieved as well. Coming to her side, Kevin slid his hand around hers.

"Josh knows you're here. He'll be down as soon as he can." He looked up at the doctor. "So what's the verdict?"

The doctor glanced down at a tablet screen briefly, more out of habit than anything else, MacKenzie thought.

"Well, we'd like to do a CT scan just to make sure there's no permanent damage. As long as that comes back okay, I think we can send her home, but someone will need to stay with her for the next twenty-four to forty-eight hours with the confusion and nausea she's dealing with. I've got a scan set up in half an hour for her, so a nurse will be here shortly to take her down."

Kevin nodded. "Thank you. How long until the confusion goes away? She seems pretty out of it."

MacKenzie shifted, uncomfortable with the two men discussing her like she was a child, but trying to think just made her head hurt worse, so she lay there quietly, grateful Kevin was there to help.

The doctor shrugged. "It really depends on her. Every person and every concussion is different, so we just have to wait and see, unfortunately. It could be hours or days or sometimes even weeks, depending on the damage. We'll know more after the scan. I'll be back to check on her when I get the results."

Kevin nodded. "Okay. Thanks."

The doctor left and MacKenzie closed her eyes, only to open them again when Kevin gently shook her shoulder.

"Hey," he said, lightly tapping her cheek. "Stay with me here. Can you talk?"

She tried to roll her eyes, though even the effort hurt enough to make her wince.

"I have a concussion," she said. "I can talk, it just...hurts. Everything pretty much hurts right now."

"Maybe I can help."

She looked past Kevin to where Josh was standing at the foot of her bed and smiled, though it quickly faded as she remembered why he was here in the first place.

"How's your dad? What happened?"

Kevin pulled back, heading for the door to make room for Josh.

"I'm just going to grab a cup of coffee," he said. "I'll be back later, K?"

MacKenzie nodded. "Thanks Kevin. For everything." He shut the door behind him and Josh moved closer, taking her hand in his.

"Is your dad okay?" she repeated. "I'm sorry I couldn't get to you..."

Josh shook his head, smoothing his free hand across her brow. "It's okay. Dad's in surgery right now - he had a heart attack and they had to open him up. Andrea's with my mom, and she'll call with any news." He frowned, looking her over.

"How did you hit your head? How are you feeling?"

She laughed, then winced. "I was looking for you and slipped on our wet floors, damn it. And I feel like I'm in a painful fog. It hurts to think, or move my head, or...anything, really. I think Kevin said something about a scan they want to do...it was hard for me to follow what the doctor said."

Josh nodded, caressing her face again. "They probably just need to make sure that brain of yours isn't bruised."

A nurse bustled in and MacKenzie glanced at her, then quickly away from the brightly patterned print of her scrub top.

"Hello, hello!" she said, her sing-song voice sending rickets of pain through MacKenzie's head. "I'm Amy. Ready for your CT scan?"

She looked at Josh, grateful for the sympathy in his somewhat amused eyes.

"I think she's ready, but can I go with her?" he asked as the nurse took her pulse and blood pressure, logging her notes into a console to the side.

"Certainly!" Amy got a couple blankets from a cupboard and held them out to Josh. "There's a wheelchair right outside the door. Why don't you put one of these on the seat, and we'll cover her up with the other. I'll help her out of bed."

MacKenzie leaned on her too-bright nurse and managed to walk to the wheelchair and settle in just as Josh's phone rang. She watched him answer and wished she could do something, anything to make everything better for him.

"It's my father," he said, giving her an apologetic look. "I have to go, I'm sorry. I'll check in as soon as I can, okay?"

She nodded, the motion hurting less than it had before, which she took as a good sign.

"Go. I'll see you later."

Amy the nurse shook her head as they watched Josh jog away. "Men. You never can count on them to be there when you need 'em." She started pushing MacKenzie in the opposite direction, and Kenzie considered arguing, but decided it would be too much work, and remained silent as Amy chattered above her all the way to radiology.

* * * * *

By the time MacKenzie got back to her room, she was pretty sure she could swing a shovel hard enough to knock Nurse Amy out cold. Unfortunately, she'd probably fall down afterward, but it was a price she was willing to pay if someone else could dig the hole.

Lucky for the far-too-cheerful nurse, they weren't near any shovels. Or likely burial spots.

Kevin was waiting in the chair beside her bed and must have noticed Kenzie's growing impatience with her caretaker. After he helped her into bed, he asked the nurse for water, and then when she got back, asked for a snack. She left quickly after her second trip, probably afraid he'd ask for something else.

"Thank you," Kenzie said, sitting up and eating her jello-pack. "I swear, people that happy shouldn't be allowed to mingle with the general population. For their own safety."

Kevin shrugged. "I'm sure she's just trying to help. Can you think of a gloomier place to work?"

Kenzie frowned, images of her drowned shop coming to mind. "An underwater comic shop."

The comment earned an eyeroll from Kevin before he glanced at the clock on the wall.

"I'm going to find your doctor, see when we can break you out of this joint, okay? Hang tight."

"Because I have so many other options?" she quipped as he headed out the door. The fogginess was abating, but her head hurt like crazy and she wanted to go home, wanted Josh, wanted everything to be just like it was twenty-four hours before.

No, scratch that. She closed her eyes and lay back on the bed, picturing that moment when Josh had kissed her. And then just after when he'd looked into her eyes and declared his intentions...she nearly sighed aloud just remembering.

That moment. That was the moment she wanted to start over at. She would have told Josh she was tired of fighting too. That she wanted to be with him, no matter what. That they'd figure everything out as they went along.

That she loved him, despite all the months they'd spent avoiding each other.

Kevin came back with the doctor and she swiped a tear from her cheek.

"Are you okay?" Kevin frowned, taking her hand. "Is the pain worse?"

She started to shake her head and then stopped. "No. It's just been a really long day." She blinked fast, and then looked up at the doctor. "Can I go home now?"

He nodded, consulting his tablet again. "I don't see anything terribly worrisome on your scans, so yes, I think home would be a much better place for you. Keep it quiet, nothing too stimulating, and don't think too hard for awhile and you should be fine, okay?"

He turned to Kevin, eyebrows raised. "You're going to stay with her for the next twenty-four hours, right?"

Kevin looked away, but squeezed her hand. "I can't...I've already missed a couple appointments today and I have somewhere I really need to be tonight. But I'll make sure someone's with her when I can't be. She won't be alone."

"Fair enough." The doctor held out a hand to shake Kevin's, and then MacKenzie's. "Come back in if your symptoms don't get better in a week or so, okay?"

"Okay." She waited until he left, and then turned to Kevin.

"Help me get dressed. I want to go see Josh."

* * * * *

"I'm not leaving yet," MacKenzie told the nurse handling her release fifteen minutes later. She was dressed and sitting on the edge of the bed, willing a wave of dizziness to subside and waiting for Kevin to take her to Josh. "There's someone I need to see first. His dad's in surgery."

The nurse sighed, leaning on the handles of the empty wheelchair she'd brought with her.

"It's hospital policy, Ms. Jones. We have to escort you to the car in a wheelchair once you've been released."

MacKenzie shook her head, immediately regretting the decision. "Can't you just escort me to that waiting room and then leave? I don't see why this is so hard. I just want to go to another part of the hospital."

"I'm sorry, but the doctor wants you to go home, so we have to see you to your car. There's no other option."

"Ready to go?" Kevin stood in the doorway, one shoulder propped against the frame as he dangled his keys in the other hand. MacKenzie started to protest, but he gave his head a small shake and winked, so after a moment's hesitation, she slowly gave a small nod.

"Sure, I guess."

She got into the wheelchair and allowed the nurse to push her behind Kevin, all the way to the front doors of the hospital. Josh's SUV was parked in one of the pick-up spots, and Kevin opened the door and helped her in, then slid behind the driver's seat as the nurse finally left them.

"This isn't your car," she said, reaching for the door handle. "What's going on? Where's Josh?"

Kevin put a hand on her wrist. "I talked to Josh before I came out to get the car. Give him a few minutes. He'll meet us here."

She let go of the handle. "But his dad..."

"Is going to be fine. He'll tell you the rest when he gets here. Just be patient, okay?"

He smiled and squeezed her shoulder. The small gesture made her want to cry as she relaxed back into the seat. They'd been friends for longer than she could remember, but she knew that sometimes she took him for granted.

"I really appreciate everything you've done for me today, Kev. Taking care of me, talking to the doctors, talking to Josh...it's just so much, and I--"

"Hey," he interrupted, taking her hand in his. "That's what friends are for, right?" He chuckled as she swiped at a tear. "Besides, you could blame this all on me, you know. I'm the one who practically ordered you to go find Josh and tell him how you feel."

She laughed. "That's true...but I'm glad you did, even with everything that happened. And I'm going to tell him, just as soon as I can."

A hand touched her shoulder through the open window, and

that personal scent she found so irresistible enveloped her in a fragrant hug.

Josh.

"Tell me what?"

* * * * *

She was cute when she was flustered, Josh thought as she looked at him with wide eyes. Not that she wasn't normally, but today, with her hair spilling down in disarray around her shoulders and eyelids at half-mast like she was trying to keep from falling asleep...it was quite possibly the sexiest thing he'd ever seen.

"Um..." she stared at him for a moment, and then turned back to Kevin, who was sliding out of the driver's seat. "Where are you going?"

"I have that thing I can't miss, remember? Josh is going to take you home and stay with you so you won't be alone. I'll check on you later." He rounded the vehicle and tossed the keys to Josh with a wink. "Take good care of our girl, okay?"

Josh nodded, grinning back. "You got it." He watched Kevin wave at MacKenzie on his way past her door and then went around and got behind the wheel. "So," he said, starting the ignition. "What did you want to tell me?"

She fidgeted in her seat as he pulled into traffic. "Maybe not while you're driving," she said after several long, silent seconds. "Kevin says your dad's going to be okay?"

He glanced at her with a sideways grin that hopefully said he'd noticed the subject change, but was going to let it slide.

"That's what the surgeon says. They put stents in his arteries, and he came out of the anesthesia okay. Andrea and Mom are going to stay with him as long as the hospital will let them. If nothing exciting happens overnight, his chances of a full recovery are very good."

"You should be with them," Kenzie said, warm concern in her voice. "I'm sure I'll be okay if you want to go back. I'm feeling much better, really."

Josh shook his head, sure she didn't realize just how tired and lost she sounded. "No way. Andrea and Mom can handle it, and they'll call if anything happens. Until tomorrow, I'm all yours."

Or forever, he added silently.

"I just hate to be such a bother," she commented. He glanced over and noted her relaxed position, head back against the seat and eyes closed. She had to be exhausted - it seemed like forever ago that they'd discovered the water leak and damage at the mall.

He pulled into his driveway and turned off the engine. She frowned when she opened her eyes.

"This isn't my house."

He nodded in agreement. "No, it's mine. But I promise you'll be cozy in my guest room, which, as I recall, you don't have. Your couch is just a little short for me, Kenzie." He grinned, enjoying the warm blush in her cheeks as she remembered the night they'd spent together.

"Point taken," she said, reaching for the door handle. "And I'm too tired to argue with you right now, so show me the bed."

He got out and hurried around the car, intending to just steady her arm as she walked. But she swayed toward him, and he scooped her up into his arms, carrying her to his door and fumbling to get his key in the lock.

"I can walk," she mumbled, her face warm against his neck,

her breath tickling his collarbone. He finally got the door open and stepped inside, not bothering to answer as he carried her down the hall to his guest room and then past it, to his own bedroom, laying her gently on one side of his bed.

If the doctor hadn't okayed her sleeping, he'd have been worried. Even with the okay, he knew he wouldn't be able to let her out of his sight for long until she was awake and coherent again.

Toeing off his shoes, he padded back out to shut and lock the front door, and then checked his phone for messages. Finding none, he went back to the bedroom and laid on the other side of the bed with as little movement as possible. She rolled to face him, still sleeping, and reached out one hand.

"Josh," she murmured, her fingers stilling as they rested against his chest, right over his heart. He put one of his hands over hers, and just laid there, watching her sleep until he couldn't keep his own eyes open any longer.

Chapter 12

MacKenzie opened her eyes to an unfamiliar room and bright sunshine filtering through semi-transparent curtains. The mattress was soft - too soft to be hers, and she was underneath a thick, cozy bedspread that wrapped around her like a hug.

Breathing in deeply, she smiled. Josh's unique, masculine scent enveloped her, reminding her of where she was, and why.

Not the way she'd planned to get into his bed, but now that she was here...

She raised her head at a sound near the foot of the bed. Josh came in the door, carrying two cups of something that smelled like coffee. She sat up, scooting back to lean against the wooden headboard.

"You're awake," he said, setting one cup down on the nightstand and carefully handing her the other. "Careful, it's hot."

"Thank you." She took a small sip, breathing in the life-giving aroma. "What time is it?"

Josh perched on the edge of the bed, facing her. "It's nearly ten. Sleep well?"

She nodded, taking another, bigger sip. "My head doesn't hurt so bad, so I must have. I'm sorry I fell asleep on you last night."

He chuckled. "I'm not. It was a long day, and we were both worn out. I was happy enough to rest up too."

Vaguely remembering a warm body in bed with her the night before, she cocked her head to the side. "Where did you sleep, exactly?"

He shrugged, reaching for his coffee and avoiding eye contact. "I didn't want to leave you alone."

She nodded, studying the machine embroidery on the duvet, all too aware of his heavy stare. "Um...thanks."

He reached out and took her cup, putting it next to his back on the nightstand. Scooting up farther on the bed, until his right leg was pressed against hers, he leaned over her legs, propping himself there with one arm as he looked into her eyes.

"What were you going to tell me yesterday, Kenzie? Kevin said that's why you hurt yourself - you were looking for me."

She looked away. "I just...well, Kevin said I was over-thinking things, and he's right." She forced herself to look at Josh, needing him to know she was sincere. "I'm tired of fighting this too, Josh. I...want you. Us. Even if--"

Josh's hand curled around her neck and pulled her forward to meet his lips, cutting off her next sentence. He tasted like fresh coffee with just a hint of mint in the background. As quickly as she'd melted into his touch, she pulled back, aghast.

"Oh, god. Morning breath. I--" She saw a split second of a grin on his lips before he claimed hers again, leaning in farther as he shifted on the bed, moving to lay beside her, urging her down to the pillows. His hands were everywhere they could reach, but there was the frustrating matter of the duvet and sheets and clothing...

MacKenzie broke free, holding him off with a firm hand to his chest and a smile when he would have pulled her back.

"Your breath is fine. Don't go."

She laughed, slipping off the other side of the bed and holding one finger up.

"I'm not going anywhere," she said, reaching down to grasp the hem of her shirt. "But there's way too much material between us, and it's driving me crazy. So strip."

* * * * *

Josh's phone rang before MacKenzie's shirt rose an inch. She stopped, and they looked at each other for a long moment while it rang again. She saw the frustration and longing she felt mirrored in his heavy gaze.

"You'd better get that," she finally said, releasing her hold on her shirt and letting it fall back in place as she sat down beside him on the bed. "Could be important."

He sat up and retrieved his phone from the nightstand, holding it to his ear.

"This is Josh."

MacKenzie felt him tense beside her, saw the color drain from his face. She reached out to put a hand on his shoulder but he pulled away and got off the bed, turning his back to her.

He spoke in low tones on the other side of the room for a minute more, and then hung up. MacKenzie wanted to go to him, but wasn't sure whether he'd welcome her comfort or not, so she stayed on the bed, wishing there was something she could do.

"Your father?"

He nodded. "Andrea said it was quick - one minute he seemed

fine, and the next his heart just stopped. They couldn't revive him."

She got up then and crossed the room, sliding a hand over his waist as she circled to stand in front of him. She pulled him into her arms and he resisted at first, but then she felt his hands slip around her waist and he hung on as though she was an anchor and he was drowning.

Tears slid down her face as she held him tight, offering what comfort she could until he slowly pulled away.

"I have to go to the hospital," he said, swiping at the tears on his own face. "I know you're not supposed to be alone, so you can come with me, or..." He got a pair of socks from the dresser and sat down to pull them on.

She shook her head, sensing that he needed time alone with his family.

"I'll come if you want, but I'll be fine by myself, really. My head doesn't hurt and I actually feel pretty normal this morning. I have my phone if I need anything. I'll be here when you get back."

"Thank you," he said, sliding his feet into a pair of loafers and pulling on a sport coat over his polo shirt. "I'll be back as soon as I can, and please, call if you need me. Seriously Kenzie. I can't lose you too."

She followed him to the front door and went up on tiptoe to press a quick, chaste kiss to his lips.

"You won't lose me. I promise. Give my condolences to your family, please."

He nodded and then he was gone, striding down the front walk with a confident cadence at odds with his drooping shoulders. She could only imagine what was going through his head, and her heart broke to see the man she loved in so much pain.

Closing and locking the door, she found her own cell phone and dialed a number she hadn't in far too long.

"Mom? It's MacKenzie."

* * * * *

MacKenzie hung up the phone half an hour later, feeling worse than she had before. She'd wanted to tell her mother about Josh, about the feelings she couldn't quite control, but as soon as her mother had heard about the flood at the shop, it was all she could focus on. Apparently it was a sign that her parents were right, and MacKenzie was wrong, and she should just give up and do something more lucrative.

When she tried to tell her about Josh, she'd chastised her for even thinking about a relationship when she couldn't even hold her business together. And then her dad had joined the conversation, trying to tell her exactly how to "fix" the mess she was in.

After unsuccessfully trying to change the subject more than once, Kenzie had given up, said her goodbyes and disconnected. And they wondered why she never called.

Not really sure what to do next, she borrowed Josh's shower, the scent of his soap and shampoo comforting. Then she made another pot of coffee and called Kevin to see how things were going at the mall. He assured her everything was being taken care of and offered to come get her, but she declined.

Wandering through Josh's domain, she noted a distinct lack of personal items. In fact aside from the bedroom, the whole place seemed like it had been decorated by a professional - not much of a stretch considering where he came from, but it definitely had more of an upscale hotel feel than somewhere to call home.

He must have a housekeeper too, she thought, noting the absence of dust on the bookshelves that held no books, but rather fake plants and a few pieces of glass and pottery artwork. She wondered if he'd picked those out, or if they came with the decorator as well.

She'd passed his office coming out from the bedroom and she went back, wondering if he'd mind her using his computer to check her email and post a note on the store's web site regarding the flood damage. The login prompt with his username stared back at her when she sat at his desk, and she frowned for a moment, wondering what he would use.

She tried Andrea's name first, and then her own, logging in on the second try. She hadn't really thought it would work, and even though she was coming to terms with the idea of them, it was still a little surreal to know he'd been thinking of her as much as she did of him.

Moving the mouse around the screen, she searched for the icon that would open a browser. There was a folder named 'Kenzie' in the upper right corner, and she frowned.

She shouldn't look. This was Josh's computer, and that had to equal journal status or something, right? She tried to think of what he might be keeping there. The mall contracts? Digital copies of her comic books? Photos of her taken on the sly?

Okay, that last one was creepy. Still, she shouldn't look. Dredging up an extreme force of willpower, she moved the mouse pointer over to the browser icon and clicked it. She logged in to check her email and responded to those that needed prompt attention. Then she logged into the comic shop's web site and put a note on the main page explaining what had happened, and telling customers to watch for details about online sales and the store renovations tomorrow.

She closed the browser, and once again that folder with her name on it was staring her in the face. The little white arrow hovered over it as of its own accord, and she wasn't even really aware of her finger clicking the button until the folder opened, and one file came up in the list, titled only "Parents".

No longer thinking about privacy, she double clicked the file to open it, and skimmed the legal document from top to bottom. It was the contract Josh's dad had used to take their house. But why would Josh want a copy of that?

When she got to the end of the document, she nearly skimmed past the signatures, but one name stood out in brilliant strong black strokes.

Sitting back in the chair, she struggled to comprehend what was right there on the screen. He should have told her. Right there at the restaurant, he could have set the record straight, but he didn't. He let her think it was his father who had basically stolen her parent's house right out from under them, when in reality, he'd been the one to sign the contract.

No wonder he'd defended his father so stridently.

She didn't bother closing the file. Just picked up the phone and called Kevin to come get her before scribbling a short note to leave on the dining room table for Josh. She wasn't cruel enough to confront him on the day his father had died, but she couldn't bear to wait for him either.

She had to go home.

* * * * *

Josh unlocked the front door and flipped on the light switch, wondering why the house was so dark. He'd been gone all day, and all he wanted now was to see MacKenzie. He'd found himself thinking of her at odd times during the day, wishing she was with him, and drawing strength just from the thought of seeing her again.

The house felt empty, and something inside him froze when he saw the folded sheet of paper on the table with his name on it in her handwriting.

She wasn't here. But where would she have gone?

He read the note, and then read it again. She thought he needed space. Time to grieve. Time to be alone. Her number was at the bottom, as if he'd been a cheap one-night stand, with the request to call in a few weeks so they could talk.

Like hell.

Letting the paper slip back to the table, he grabbed his keys and wallet again and went out the front door, slamming it shut behind him. He wasn't sure what had gone wrong this time, but he couldn't let her just walk away again. Not today.

Half an hour later he knocked on her door, and then knocked again when no one answered. The lights were on, and a shadow had moved across the window more than once, so he knew someone was in there.

"Kenzie, open up. It's Josh."

He waited a few more minutes, and then knocked again.

"If you don't open up, I'm calling the cops to open this door for a medical emergency. You're not supposed to be left alone yet. I need to know you're okay."

A few seconds later, he heard the deadbolt click back and the door opened just enough so he could see her tired, frustrated expression.

"What the hell happened?" he asked. "Why did you leave?"

"I'm fine, Josh. Go back to your family. We'll talk later."

He shook his head. "No. If we need to talk, we do it now. I've lost one person I love today, and I'm not doing it again. Let me come in and you can tell me about whatever's bothering you. But I'm not walking away again. And I'm not letting you walk away either. We're done with games, remember? Talk to me."

She lowered her gaze...or was she blinking back tears? He reached out to life her chin, but she pulled away. Moving back, she opened the door and waited for him to come inside before closing and locking it again.

"Okay." She led him into the small, cozy living room and took a seat in one of the armchairs. He sat on the couch and leaned forward to brace his elbows on his knees, his heart heavy for whatever he'd done this time to put that deep hurt in her eyes.

She regarded him with glassy eyes for a long moment before she finally spoke. "Let's talk about your role in your dad's company, and the contract you - not him - signed to steal my parent's property."

Chapter 13

MacKenzie expected him to deny it. To demand an explanation of how she found out. She was ready for it, ready to argue. Ready for a loud, drawn out fight - hell, maybe she even wanted one. Something to release all the hurt and anger that had been building since she saw the contract on his computer.

Josh didn't say anything for a long moment. He just leaned back against the couch cushions and sighed, finally meeting her gaze with a tired, resigned look.

"It was a long time ago, Kenzie. I honestly didn't even remember signing it until I pulled up the contract after we went out that first time. I wanted to see what the details were, to see if there was anything I could do. When I saw my signature, I knew I should tell you but then we stopped talking, and it didn't matter anymore."

She shook her head, swiping at angry tears. "And you thought it still wouldn't matter when you told me I should stop fighting my feelings for you? It didn't matter when you kissed me in the office? You didn't think I'd want to know before I finally decided to give in to...us?"

He looked down at his hands, his shoulders slumped, and she had to remind herself not to feel sorry for him. She'd tried to wait. Tried to let him grieve before they dealt with this. He's the one who chose to come over and force her hand.

"I didn't think about the contract, or your parents, or my parents, or anything else when I kissed you, Kenzie. I just knew I needed you more than anything else. Nothing else mattered...just you."

She flopped back in her own chair. "Yeah. Well. It would have mattered to me. It mattered then, and it matters now." She waited until he met her eyes again. "Are you going to take over for your dad, now that he's gone?"

He shrugged. "I don't know yet, but I'll have to for a little while, at least. I can't just let it fall apart. It's our family's legacy. And it supports us - all of us, even Andrea's shop. My family depends on that income."

Kenzie rubbed a hand across her face and then stood, blinking back tears as she looked down at him.

"You know how I feel about that business, Josh. And if you still don't see the issue with turning people out on the street to make a buck, this is never going to work between us, because I just can't be with someone who would do that. I just can't. Have a nice life - and lock the door on your way out."

Side-stepping the hand he held out, she ran down the hall to her bedroom and locked herself in, letting the tears fall even as she pressed a hand against her mouth to stay quiet. His footsteps came down the hall, stopped in front of her door. But he didn't knock.

She listened to him walk away, heard the front door close. And despite everything she'd said - and truly believed - her heart shattered at the sound of him walking out of her life for good.

The next few weeks went by in a blur. MacKenzie stayed busy with the store remodel and reopening as well as all the administrative duties running the mall required. Josh was absent most of the time, dealing with his father's affairs and business, she assumed. When she did catch a brief glimpse of him at the catering shop or in the back office, she stayed away. It was too painful to be near him - wanting him, yet knowing she'd hate herself if she compromised her beliefs to be with him.

Andrea had supplied a generous spread of finger foods for the reopening, though she sent her staff over to deliver it rather than bringing it over herself. When Kenzie tried to thank her in person, Andrea was unavailable even though Kenzie could clearly see her through the window behind the front counter that looked into the kitchen of Taste the World.

The woman looked up, briefly meeting Kenzie's gaze with a cold stare before turning her back completely.

Kenzie stifled a sigh, and turned back to the woman behind the counter who was clearly a little worried by the exchange.

"You'd better let me pay for the treats she sent over. How much is the damage?" Kenzie got her personal credit card out of her wallet and hoped she'd still have enough left for groceries. Insurance had covered most, but not all of the damages, and she'd had to kick in the rest to finish the restocking. It would be canned beans and ramen for a few more weeks, at least.

The woman hit a few keys and finally frowned at the screen in front of her.

"Your order was paid for up front. You don't owe anything."

Kenzie rolled her eyes. "You mean she didn't invoice it. Can you just estimate what I'd owe? I can describe the dishes, if that helps."

"You don't understand." The woman shook her head. "The order was placed and paid for the same day. Andrea invoiced it, and…" she peered closer at the screen, tapping a few more keys. "It looks like Josh paid for it. So you're all set!" She grinned, obviously relieved that there wasn't a problem after all.

But there was.

Kenzie smiled, playing along. "Can you tell me how much it was, please? For my tax records, of course."

"Sure. It was--" The woman rattled off a number that had Kenzie grasping at the edge of the counter to maintain her balance. She almost asked how that could possibly be right, but the woman looked so calm that Kenzie just nodded and forced a wan smile while her stomach turned.

"Thank you," she said, working at an air of nonchalance as she walked out - and positive she was failing miserably. Back at her desk in the comic shop, she sat and stared at the inventory shelves on the wall in front of her, various thoughts swirling around in her head.

Josh had paid full price to provide treats for her opening - but why? Why hadn't Andrea given him a break on the price, considering he was family? And if she had, that made it even worse.

She rubbed a hand over her forehead, shaking her head. She couldn't let him do this - couldn't be indebted to him for something she hadn't even asked for. Especially given the state of their relationship. She had to pay him back. And he wasn't taking no for an answer, even though she'd have to make payments for a couple months.

Slinging her purse over her shoulder and grabbing her keys, she left Trevor to close the shop and went to her car, her heart beating a million miles a minute at the very thought of talking to him again. She sat in the car for a few minutes, just breathing and telling herself to calm down. She could do this. She needed to do this. He had to understand that he couldn't buy her off. What she needed from him was far more important than money, and something she didn't think he'd ever be able to give.

Opening her eyes, she put her seatbelt on and turned the key in the ignition. One more deep breath, and she drove out of the parking lot, heading for his house.

* * * * *

Fifteen minutes later, MacKenzie wasn't sure what to say. Sitting outside Josh's place, she went over all the things she wanted to tell him, but nothing sounded right in her head.

Probably because the only thing she really wanted to say was that she loved him, and wanted him back.

She rubbed a hand down the side of her face and then got her wallet out of her purse. The amount she could spare was paltry, but it would have to do as a token amount. She just had to stay strong, and not take no as an answer.

Getting out of the car, she closed the door and went up the front walk, hesitating only a moment before she knocked on the door. Footsteps on the other side made her pulse race even faster and she prayed she wouldn't do...or say anything too stupid.

The door swung open and Kenzie opened her mouth, only to close it again with a frown.

"Can I help you?"

The woman was tall, even taller in four-inch spike heels, and dressed for a night on the town in a slim black sheath. Her blond hair was piled on top of her head in a way that would have just looked messy on Kenzie, but managed to look sexily tousled on this woman with a few ringlets just casually hanging down here and there.

Her complexion was flawless - the makeup, no doubt since no one was naturally that perfect. Her smile was sincere and patient, her eyes annoyingly intelligent.

MacKenzie blew her hair out of her eyes with a puff from her lips, knowing instinctively that she'd lost this battle before it even started. Of course he wouldn't just wait around for her. A strong, attractive, well-off man like Josh could land any beauty he wanted, and this woman looked like some gorgeous executive who'd just happened to do a little modeling for spare change in college.

In MacKenzie's experience, brains could sometimes best beauty, but it was impossible to beat the full package. The blond was talking again, and she chided herself to pay attention. Give Josh the money, let him know she'd pay him back, and get out. That's all she needed to do. Purely business.

"If you need to use the phone, you can borrow mine..."

Kenzie shook her head. "No thank you," she said, relieved when her voice didn't crack. "I actually just need to talk to Josh for a minute. Is he here?"

The woman nodded. "I'll get him - just a moment. Can I tell him your name?"

"Tell him MacKenzie's here."

Leaving the door slightly ajar, the woman disappeared, and Kenzie could almost hear the clock ticking as she waited. Maybe she shouldn't do this in person. Maybe she should just write a note, and send him the money. She couldn't very well make a scene in front of his date...or she could, but it was one thing to yell at Josh in private, and quite another to air their dirty laundry in front of someone who looked like she'd never lost her temper in her life.

Turning away, MacKenzie went down the steps. She'd mail him his money, and a frigid little note to let him know exactly how she felt about him paying her way when they weren't even...

"Kenzie? Did you need to see me?"

She froze at the sound of his voice behind her and took a deep breath. Frigid. She could do frigid in person, even if the mere smell of him on the breeze heated her body by several degrees.

Turning, she gave him a curt nod, and held out the bills she'd taken out of her purse.

"Yes - sorry. I'll be quick. I can't let you pay for the finger foods Andrea made for my re-opening. Here's the first installment - I'll pay you back every dime, it's just going to take me a few months. Please don't do that again. I don't need your charity."

* * * * *

Josh ignored the bills she held. "How did you find out it was me?"

Andrea had promised MacKenzie wouldn't find out who had paid for her opening day catering. He'd known Kenzie wouldn't accept his help, and he'd also known she couldn't afford the cost on her own - especially since Andrea refused to give her a break when Josh told her the reason they weren't seeing each other. He'd thought his sister would be sympathetic, having stated some of the same concerns Kenzie had about the family business, but her loyalty had trumped any common ground between the two women, and nothing Josh could say would change that.

"It doesn't matter." Kenzie slapped the bills against his chest and released them, stepping back as they fluttered to the ground.

"I don't need your money, and I don't want you doing things for me. It implies that we have certain type of rela--"

"It implies that I care about you, and I think you're well aware of that, regardless of the fact that we're having a rough patch. But I have a pla--"

"A rough patch?" She laughed, an ugly sound of disbelief as she rolled her eyes. "You call this a rough patch? More like irreconcilable differences, I'd say. Besides, it looks like you're moving on just fine. I have to go."

He sighed. "Kenzie, wait. It's not what you think." As expected, she kept walking, and he knew there was nothing he could do to make her stop.

"It never is." Her quiet, hurt words drifted back to him on the breeze, and he wished she'd let him explain. But maybe it would be better to wait. In a few days when everything was finalized, he'd be able to show her the contracts as proof. It wouldn't solve all of their problems, but he hoped it would be a start.

"She seems pretty upset. I'm guessing she has something to do with why you decided to reorganize the firm?"

He nodded as Jennifer came down the stairs to stand beside him as he watched MacKenzie drive away.

"In a way," he said, not interested in divulging any more than necessary about his personal life. The only reason he'd had Jennifer meet him at his house was to avoid anyone at the office getting a whiff of what he was doing before it was finalized. That MacKenzie would show up had never crossed his mind.

Just one more thing for her to be mad about, though if she'd just given him a minute to explain…

"What time is it?"

She checked her watch. "Late. We'd better go."

He turned back to the house. "Just let me grab the file and I'll follow you to the restaurant. Did you reserve the conference room in the back?"

Jennifer nodded, her heels already clicking toward her car. "It's all set. I'll wait for you in the parking lot."

Josh waved her off and got the file he needed, then drove to the restaurant. He waited for the anxiety and guilt to take hold, knowing his dad wouldn't approve of this move at all, but the feelings that had plagued him on and off for the past several weeks were decidedly absent. Taking that as a good sign, he got out of his car, let Jennifer straighten his tie, and went to meet with the new managers who would start reorganizing his entire company first thing in the morning.

Chapter 14

MacKenzie went straight from Josh's house to the grocery store in her neighborhood and bought a clamshell pack of her favorite frosted sugar cookies and a chilled bottle of Riesling. Once home, she poured herself a glass and took the bottle and the entire package of cookies to the living room, curling up on the sofa with her favorite throw and an old movie.

She'd realized as soon as Josh came out of the house that there was nothing going on between him and the blond. Or if there was, it wasn't anything of substance - she hadn't detected any tension or chemistry between them at all. But it had given her an easy excuse to walk away - better him think she was jealous than to know that it was just too painful to stay close to him for even one minute longer.

Pressing the money against his chest had been foolish, to say the least. Touching him, feeling his heat come through his clothes, the tension between them so taut it felt like it would burst any second...

She'd had to get out of there before she did anything stupid. Like fling herself into his arms and kiss him senseless, begging him to take her back.

God, what an idiot.

She polished off another cookie and washed it down with a

healthy swig of wine, glancing at the TV and realizing she had no idea what she was even watching. Turning the screen off, she tossed the remote on the coffee table and helped herself to another cookie. She'd regret it in the morning - all that sugar and alcohol without any real substance would undoubtedly give her one heck of a hangover, but she didn't care. Snuggling down deeper into the cushions and pulling the blanket tighter around her body, she closed her eyes and drifted into a fantasy world where she and Josh could finally be together.

When the doorbell rang, her eyes flew open and for a moment, she wasn't sure where she was. The empty wineglass and cookie crumbs on the table jogged her memory even as the doorbell rang again. She frowned, holding one hand to her head as she checked the clock on the DVR. Two in the morning? It had to be either an emergency or a really horrible prank.

Padding to the door, she reached it just as the doorbell pealed again.

"Who is it?" she yelled, not bothering to temper the annoyance in her voice. Maybe they'd just go away.

"It's Josh."

She turned, bracing her back against the door and reminding herself to breathe. What the hell was he doing here, and so late? It had to be an emergency with the mall, she decided. He had no other reason to stop by at this time of night.

Fumbling with the deadbolt, she pulled the door open and looked up into his face.

"Did the water line break again? Did you call the recovery company? I'm pretty sure they said their services were guaranteed..."

"Nothing's wrong at the mall, Kenz." Josh shook his head, and she noticed he was holding a thick manila envelope in his hand.

"Why are you here then?" She raised her eyebrows, propping herself up on the door and trying to look more normal than she felt.

He held the file out to her. "Two things. First, this is for you. I want you to know what I decided to do with my father's company - it's all there."

She took the envelope, surprised at the weight. "Okay. And the second thing?"

One corner of his mouth quirked up in a small smile, and then before she could blink, he leaned in and placed an easy, gentle kiss on her lips.

"I love you, MacKenzie. And I don't care what I have to do or how long I have to wait. I'm not giving up on you. On us. If those papers don't prove that, I don't know what will."

He turned and walked away, his kiss and that declaration leaving her shaky and needy and weak in the knees. The motions automatic, she locked the door and made her way to the couch, setting the file on the coffee table. She poured a half-glass of wine from the now-warm bottle and tossed it back as she contemplated the envelope and what its contents could possibly mean.

After a few deep breaths, she reached out with shaky hands and took the papers out of their wrapping, leaning back against the cushions to read.

* * * * *

Bright sunlight woke MacKenzie the next morning as it filtered through the semi-transparent curtains in her living room. Pushing up from the awkward and somewhat painful position she'd fallen asleep in, she rubbed her face with her hands and groaned, her head spinning.

"Ow, dammit," she said to the empty room, the sound of her own voice making her cringe. What the hell had she been thinking, finishing off that whole bottle by herself?

Catching sight of the empty cookie carton, she started to shake her head, stopping when the movement sent searing pain through her temples. So much for all those late nights in college. She was officially a lightweight, she chided herself.

Forcing herself to stand, she grabbed the empty bottle and the carton, turning to take them into the kitchen. Stepping down on something crinkly and definitely not carpet, she slowly looked down as it all came tumbling back.

The knock at the door. The sheaf of papers.

That kiss that had quite literally made her weak in the knees.

She put the bottle and carton back down on the coffee table and sank to the couch, reaching down to pick the papers off the floor. Shuffling them back into order, she stared for a long time at the first page.

Essentially a mission statement, the three-page document stated that Josh was restructuring the tax lien company into a financial advisory foundation for people who had defaulted on their property taxes or other debt and needed help. Rather than negotiating with companies on the debtor's behalf, Josh's company would teach people how to be their own negotiators, empowering them to get out of debt faster and smarter, and to avoid losing their homes or properties.

There were contracts included, and a bunch of legal mumbo-jumbo that MacKenzie skimmed through, but she did note that the foundation would be funded through both private family money and donations from wealthy benefactors. So it wouldn't cost customers a dime, unless they chose to donate later.

She wanted to believe it was sincere, but what if he'd only done it for her? And how did his family feel about the whole thing? Would they hate her for being the catalyst that caused this massive disruption of the family business? And how would the new foundation stay solvent without a regular influx of cash?

Putting the papers back on the table, she retrieved the bottle and cookie carton again, taking them to the garbage. Then she got a Coke from the fridge and padded down the hall to the bathroom for a shower. There was only one way to find out the answers to her questions, and this time, she wasn't going to run away, no matter how heated or uncomfortable things got.

She had no idea what she'd do if he wasn't sincere, but she'd worry about it then.

Unable to stop thinking about seeing him again, she didn't linger under the hot water like she normally did, but got out, dried off, and dressed in record time. Grabbing her keys, purse, and the paperwork from the coffee table, she flung herself out into the hallway and raced down the stairs.

* * * * *

MacKenzie's heart beat faster as she made her way through the dark, cozy warren that made up the tax lien offices Josh had inherited. Lush green carpet muffled her footsteps as she peered into the glass and dark wood interior walls at people hastily packing cardboard boxes with all their personal possessions - and maybe a stapler or two.

The documents she'd read hadn't said anything about firing

people, only restructuring the company. But it looked as though a good percentage of the staff was packing up to leave permanently. That couldn't be a good sign.

She took a left down another short hall where more people were packing up, and then a right into the lobby where two desks faced each other on either side of two massive wooden doors with Taylor, the family name, embossed in the center of each.

One of the desks was in the process of being cleaned out by a younger, distraught-looking woman who didn't even glance MacKenzie's way. At the other desk sat an older lady with a stern expression who peered over thin reading glasses at MacKenzie.

"Can I help you?" The words were cordial enough, but it was all Kenzie to could do not to shiver and rub her arms at the sub-zero tone.

She forced herself to move closer, and smile politely. "I need to speak with Josh Taylor, please."

"He's not here. And as you can see..." the woman nodded pointedly at the girl who'd almost finished packing.

"We're a little busy today. I can make you an appointment for next week if you'd like, but he may not be able to keep it."

"I'll just catch up with him later," Kenzie said, watching the other woman pick up her box of things and walk out. "It kind of looks like you're closing down, actually. Why's everyone leaving?"

The secretary frowned, giving her a closer look. "What did you say your name was, again?"

Kenzie thought about playing coy, but it was pretty clear that this woman had already guessed that she wasn't just any old customer, and it must be a good sign that she wasn't packing up like so many others.

"I'm MacKenzie Jones. Nice to meet you." She held out her hand, a little surprised when the other woman shook it and actually gave her a small smile.

"He mentioned you might stop by. He also said to tell you he was going to Taste the World, and you could catch up with him there, if you want."

Kenzie nodded. "I'll head over there now, thank you. I appreciate it." She turned to go, only getting a few steps before the woman spoke again.

"You're a very lucky woman, you know. When a man basically turns his whole life upside down for you, you know he's a keeper."

Kenzie half-turned to meet the woman's earnest stare. "I didn't want him to do it for me though. I wanted him to do it for him."

That actually earned her a laugh. "Honey, no man would make such an expensive change without some serious soul-searching. Sometimes they just need a good hard shove in the right direction, and you gave him that. He wouldn't have acted on it if he didn't think it was the right thing to do."

Kenzie managed to nod before she walked out, making her way back through the warren to the front desk, and on into the parking lot. Sliding behind the wheel, she just sat for a few moments, watching people flow in and out of the building like so many ants.

From the looks of it, Josh was losing over half his staff, though she wasn't sure whether he'd fired them, or if they were leaving voluntarily. The documents he'd given her were basically a blueprint for turning the company into the antithesis of what his dad had built over the years. And now that she thought about it, his secretary was right. It was really kind of silly to think he'd do something that would cause so much upheaval and profit loss to so many just because of...her.

She had to find him.

The mall was fifteen minutes away but she made it in ten, parking in front of Andrea's shop. Taste the World wouldn't open for another hour, but she knew someone would be in the back, baking. Hopefully that's where Josh would be too. She took out her keys and walked to the front door, her nose wrinkling instinctively at the smell of something burning.

Cupping one hand against the glass, she peered inside, panic rising in her throat when she saw smoke billowing out of the kitchen over the pass-through window to the front counter.

* * * * *

Struggling with both her keys and her phone, MacKenzie finally fitted the master key in the lock while she dialed 9-1-1. She pulled the door open, smoke flowing out steadily as the operator came online.

"9-1-1, what's your emergency?"

"There's a fire at Taste the World. 1539 Highgate Drive. There's a lot of smoke..." MacKenzie choked back a cough, turning her head away for a second.

"Okay ma'am, I've dispatched a fire truck to your location. They're ten minutes away. Is there anyone inside? And where are you now?"

"Two people, at least. And I'm in the doorway," she said, squinting as she tried to see through the white cloud. A strong breeze seemed to pull a bunch of smoke out at once, and in the brief moment before the front of the store filled again, she saw a large male hand stretched out toward her on the floor near the counter.

"Josh?" she called, taking a step forward and getting a lungful of smoke for her efforts. "Josh, can you hear me?"

The emergency operator was saying something, but Kenzie had already put the phone down. She grabbed a nearby loose brick and propped open the door, putting her cell on the ground. She pulled the front of her shirt up over her mouth and nose before running inside, dimly aware of voices and sirens growing louder behind her.

When she reached him, Josh was unconscious and lying on his back, his head facing the door as if he'd been trying to get out. She grabbed both arms and pulled, but nothing happened.

"Dammit." She choked back tears and tried again, throwing every bit of her strength into moving the man, but he wouldn't budge.

Then someone squeezed her shoulder, and she turned to find Matt from the bike shop beside her.

"I'll get one, you get the other. Ready?"

She nodded, grasping Josh's arm closest to her. "Let's go."

It took everything she had, but they pulled him out of the store to the sidewalk just as a big fire truck pulled in. Kenzie knelt by his side, one hand on his chest and the other feeling for a pulse at his neck.

"Josh? Can you hear me? Please wake up...please be okay..."

"Move aside please, ma'am." Someone with a strong grip grabbed her arms and pulled her away, the paramedics immediately taking her place. She shrugged out of Matt's hold as a fireman approached.

"Are you the woman who called it in?"

She nodded, watching more firemen aim a hose at the roof. No one was going through the door though, and panic shot through her.

"Did you find Andrea? She's probably in there...you have to find her. In the kitchen." She started toward the door, her only thought to save Josh's sister. When Matt grabbed her again, holding her back, she fought.

"Let me go! I have to go help her!"

The fireman stood in front of them, one hand on her shoulder and the other on the radio mic clipped to his shoulder.

"There's a woman inside. Do we have someone in there?"

The reply was garbled, and Kenzie wasn't listening anyway. She tore free from Matt's hold and ducked the fireman's arm, sprinting toward the door of the shop as fast as she could. Shouts and yells erupted all around as she flung herself back into the dark, smoke-filled shop.

Andrea had to be there somewhere. Kenzie guessed she'd been following Josh out, so she went toward the counter, pushing display tables out of her way whenever she encountered one, and feeling completely disoriented and a little woozy as she wandered through the thick haze. What if she was going the wrong way? What if she got lost herself, and passed out? Would they find her in time?

Lightheaded and more than a little dizzy, she pressed on, relieved when she finally ran into the long counter at the back of the store. The sound was surprisingly loud, with fire crackling ahead of her and some sort of scuffling behind her. Something in the back of her mind told her to get down on the floor, so she did, placing one hand against the base of the counter as she found the end and crawled toward the kitchen.

Her eyes and lungs burned, her chest heavier with every breath as she moved forward. When her hand finally touched what felt like human skin, she nearly cried with relief.

She found both arms and grasped Andrea's wrists, wishing for a deep breath to help her pull. Standing up, she took a single excruciating step backwards, and then another, and another, relieved that Josh's sister was a far cry lighter than he was.

It seemed like an eternity before she bumped into another human. Thick, canvas-covered arms wrapped tight around her waist and pulled her back, forcing her to let go of Andrea. She struggled for a moment, until another tan-bundled man stepped in and picked Andrea up.

She tried to take another breath, but the air was gone. Everything went dark.

Chapter 15

His throat felt like it was on fire when Josh woke up, and his eyes burned so badly he couldn't suppress a slight groan when he opened them. Panic gripped him as he remembered the fire and how he'd fallen trying to get himself and Andrea out. Moving restlessly, he winced at the pains shooting through his head.

A gentle touch on his left arm was unexpected, but welcome and some of the fear ebbed out of him.

"Shh...it's okay. You're safe now. Just relax."

The soft, feminine voice was soothing and familiar, and he settled, closing his eyes again. Maybe she was an angel sent to guide him to heaven. Or to watch over him while he died.

He hoped not. There was so much that he still wanted to do, and he had to see MacKenzie. He had to tell her he loved her again, and make sure she believed it.

"I'm here, Josh. I won't leave, I promise."

He drifted off again, and the next time he opened his eyes, the room was dim, but clearer. His throat didn't hurt as badly, and he shifted on the bed, his hand brushing against something soft and silky. He glanced down as MacKenzie lifted her head from the mattress, blinking sleep from her eyes as she pushed the hair out of her face. The moment she realized he was awake, her eyes widened and a smile spread over her face.

"You're awake." She stood up and moved closer, grasping one of his hands in hers. "How do you feel?"

He shrugged, even that small motion somewhat painful. "I'm okay, I think. Sore from laying here. How long have I been out?" His throat was dry, and he would have asked for water, but Kenzie was already reaching for a cup on a nearby table. She held it up so he could reach the straw, steadying it as he took a long drink.

"It's been most of the day," she said, putting the cup back down. "The doctor said the smoke was really bad. You and Andrea almost didn't make it."

Josh tried to sit up, panic coursing through him again. "Andrea - is she okay? Where is she?"

"She's okay, or she will be." MacKenzie gently pushed him back down. "You two both got a good dose of carbon monoxide in the smoke from the fire. That's why you're on oxygen, and so is she. She hasn't woke up yet, but the doctors are optimistic. Do you remember how the fire started?"

He stared at the ceiling, trying to remember. "We were arguing." He frowned at the memory. "She was making something - I don't remember what, but she was caramelizing sugar, so probably using one of those little blow torches. I said something, she turned to argue with me, and the next thing I know, a towel caught on fire. I tossed it in the sink to get it away from the stove, but there was a jar of grease on the counter that got knocked over, and the next thing we knew, the whole place was filled with smoke. I was trying to pull Andrea out, but she wouldn't leave, and I hit the counter and fell..." he looked at Kenzie again. "That's the last thing I remember. How did we get out?"

Kenzie looked down at her hands, fidgeting. "You weren't at your office, and your secretary said you were with Andrea. So I went to the shop and saw the smoke..." she shook her head, as if trying to shake off a bad memory.

Josh put a hand on hers and squeezed. "Thank God you came when you did. And that the fire department got there quickly too. Do you know who pulled Andrea and I out? We'll need to thank them, Andrea and I."

Kenzie's cheeks turned pink, and she hesitated. "Josh, I--"

The door to his room opened and a nurse bustled in, his mother right behind her.

"Son, you're awake! I was so worried. How do you feel? Where does it hurt? Your sister just woke up a few minutes ago too - they're checking her out now."

Josh lost his hold on Kenzie as his mother pushed in and MacKenzie moved back to make room. He winced as his mother hugged him, and Kenzie gave him a slight smile and wiggled her fingers in a little wave before she slipped out the door.

* * * * *

Out in the hall, MacKenzie allowed herself a deep, reviving breath. As soon as the doctors had released her to go, she'd found Josh and refused to leave his side until he woke up, much to his mother's chagrin. Eventually she'd left MacKenzie to sit with Josh while she went to Andrea's side.

Kenzie wasn't sure why she was reluctant to tell Josh that she'd tried to save him and failed. Without Matt's help, they'd both be dead, so really the credit all went to him. And she'd already been lectured by the paramedics, the fire chief and

Josh's mom for going back in after Andrea. Apparently her attempts to help had just made everyone else's job more complicated, and she was pretty much feeling like the ultimate failure by the time she'd fallen asleep at Josh's side.

Deep down, she figured she didn't want to hear Josh lecture her too. Even out of concern.

She moved down the wide hall to Andrea's room, wanting to see for herself that Andrea was awake and okay. The door was open and she went in, smiling at the woman lying in bed, her eyes open and alert.

"I just wanted to see how you were doing," she said, stopping near the foot of the bed. "Josh is awake too. He's going to be okay."

"That's good." Andrea nodded, but her tone was curt. Kenzie wasn't sure what to say after that, but she wanted to help if she could.

"Kevin said he'd make sure the shop is locked up and taken care of while you're out. I'm sure he'll stop by tomorrow. He was pretty worried about you."

Andrea rolled her eyes. "I don't know why he'd be worried about me. We haven't spoken in weeks. Tell him not to bother. I don't want to see him." She looked Kenzie in the eye. "I really don't want to see you either, honestly. None of this would have happened if it weren't for you."

MacKenzie frowned, folding her arms across her chest. "I wasn't anywhere near the mall when the fire star--"

"Not just the fire," Andrea said, her face red and her voice raspy. "Everything. Ever since you opened your ridiculous little store in the mall beside us, my brother's been falling all over himself to get to you. And you've strung him along this whole time, finding any excuse you could not to be with him, and then reeling him in just when he was finally starting to see some sense. Which would have been bad enough if it was just that, but no, you had to drag our father's business into it. And now Josh has made this grand gesture of turning everything our father built, the business our family depended on, upside down, just for you. That business was backup funding for my shop, MacKenzie. No family business, no rebuilding. No reopening. No more Taste the World. Understand?"

MacKenzie nodded, slowly and looked away, not wanting Andrea to see the tears in her eyes.

"I'm sorry," she said, turning to go. "I honestly never meant to hurt anyone. I...love your brother, and I hope that someday you can forgive me for the hurt I've caused you."

She walked out the door and back toward Josh's room, where his mother was still fawning over him. As much as she longed to be with him right now, she didn't think she could go through another confrontation with his mom right now. She needed sleep, and a shower, and something to eat, not necessarily in that order. She'd come back and talk to Josh tomorrow, when they were all more awake and alert.

Turning away, she asked one of the nurses to call her a cab, and then went down to the front lobby to wait.

* * * * *

When she got home, MacKenzie put her cell phone and keys on the counter, ignoring the blinking light that told her messages were waiting. Knowing she should eat something even though she wasn't really hungry, she downed an oatmeal bar with a glass of milk standing at the kitchen counter. After a quick shower, she crawled into bed. Exhausted, depressed, and alone, she finally let the tears come.

She woke to loud, incessant knocking at the front door. A sharp pain dove through her head like a steel spike as she pulled her groggy self out of bed and stumbled to the living room. As she got closer to the door, she could hear someone calling her name from the other side. It took a few seconds for her fogged brain to process the voice as she pulled the door open.

"Josh?"

He didn't say anything, just gathered her up in a tight hug and the next thing she knew, her feet weren't touching the ground, her door slammed shut behind them and she was up against the wall with his warm body pressing against her everywhere, his lips devouring her as though she was his last meal.

On some level she knew she should object, should insist on talking things out, but she was tired of talking. Tired of fighting and trying to make everything make sense. She wanted this, wanted to quit thinking and just feel, just be with the man she loved and forget about everything else. It could fall into place or not, as it would, but this...this was good. This would never be wrong.

Sliding her hands around his neck and locking her ankles at his back, she returned his kisses, feeling his lips turn up in a smile at her acquiescence.

"I love you," she breathed, needing to say it, needing him to hear the words, no matter what else happened. He kissed her again, and again, moving across her jaw line and playfully nipping her earlobe.

"I love you too." His husky timbre sent shivers of desire

through her body, and she held on tight as he carried her to her bedroom. He sat on the bed and she pulled his shirt over his head before pushing him down to his back, and then pulled her shirt off too, flinging it across the room.

She'd only worn panties and a t-shirt to bed, and with the shirt gone, she was bare for his gaze. He looked up at her, his hands caressing her ribs and moving to cup her breasts, his thumbs teasing her nipples into turgid peaks.

She rocked her hips, earning a groan and he reached up to grasp the back of her neck and pull her down for more kisses. Then she was on her back, kicking her panties off while he shucked his pants and donned a condom.

He settled between her legs and kissed her again, his eyes never leaving hers as he slid home in one smooth thrust.

Finally. MacKenzie reached up and cupped his face with one hand, feeling more whole, more complete than she ever had in her life. She wanted to tell him how she felt, tell him how much he meant, how she never wanted to be without him again, but words just seemed so...inadequate.

He nodded as though he understood, and then began to move within her. It was the most exquisite feeling, and she arched up, her hips catching the rhythm of his as the tension between them pulled tighter and tighter, until it finally snapped, the release sending waves of intense pleasure throughout her body, the incredible sensation fogging her mind.

It was several minutes before either of them moved, and when Josh finally did, she wanted to protest. Instead she lay there wondering what she should do. Get up? Stay in bed? Talk to him about...everything? Doubt and insecurity threatened to flood out the pleasure until he came back and crawled between the covers with her, tugging her back close to his front and wrapping her up in his warmth.

"Stop thinking," he murmured in her ear. "Let's just rest for awhile, and then we'll figure everything else out, okay?"

She nodded. Smiled as a sense of calm settled over her. Snuggled in closer and closed her eyes, trusting that everything would be okay, now that he was with her.

"Okay."

* * * * *

The next time Kenzie woke she was alone, and for a moment she wondered if she'd dreamed the whole encounter with Josh. Sitting up, she pushed her hair out of her eyes and yawned, noting the light coming through the windows and wondering what time it was. Sliding out of bed she got dressed and brushed her teeth before padding barefoot out to the kitchen for coffee.

There was a full pot on the counter, and she poured herself a cup, her lips curving up in a grin as she went to go look for Josh.

Her grin faded when she found him in the living room with Andrea.

He smiled as if nothing was wrong and came to her, placing a gentle kiss on her lips.

"I'm glad you're up. I didn't want to wake you, but Andrea has something she'd like to discuss with us."

MacKenzie followed him to the couch and sat beside him, eyeing his sister warily. She looked much better than the last time Kenzie had seen her in the hospital, though her eyes were still colder than Kenzie would have liked. She supposed this was where Andrea tried to break them up for good. She took a big gulp of coffee, steeling herself against whatever barbs the woman might start throwing.

"I said some things to you in the hospital yesterday I shouldn't have said," Andrea began. MacKenzie raised her eyebrows, not entirely sure the other woman was sincere.

Andrea shrugged. "I still don't agree with how you've treated my brother, or how you keep pushing him away, or even how he thinks he wants to be with you--"

"Andrea." Josh interrupted, and Kenzie glanced at him. His expression was blank, but his tone was firm. "You don't approve - we get it. Just get to the point. Tell her your proposal."

Andrea rolled her eyes, and then seemed to regroup, looking back at Kenzie.

"I was going over the books last night, and I think we have nearly enough money in our accounts for the major repairs to the kitchen. That still leaves us several thousand short on operating capitol though, and Kevin suggested a fund-raising campaign and silent auction to raise the last bit of money we need. That's where you come in. We hope."

MacKenzie nodded. "Go on."

"Kevin suggested auctioning off some of the older collectible comics you have at your store." Andrea held a hand up when MacKenzie would have protested. "I told him I couldn't do that. But what if there was a new comic book in development? One that our customers could bid on to be featured in as characters, either ongoing or one-time, depending on the amount they bid or donate? Kevin said we could produce them independently and sell them in our shop, and our business customers could buy advertising slots. Kevin said he'd write it for us, pro bono at first, and then as we get back on our feet, we'll work out a payment plan of some sort."

MacKenzie nodded. It was a long shot, but if they could get the word out and write a good storyline, it could work.

"So what do you need from me?" she asked.

Andrea smiled. "We'd like...well, we were hoping you'd illustrate it. And I know it's a lot to ask, but we obviously can't pay you, so it would be a donation."

MacKenzie looked at Josh, and he seemed to know what she was thinking.

"This has nothing to do with you and I, Kenzie. It won't affect my feelings for you either way, so don't feel like you have to say yes."

She nodded, appreciating that, even though she knew it wasn't the whole truth. Still, she wanted to help, and this...this was something she could do, even if she wasn't entirely sure it would work as well as they hoped.

"Okay. I'm in. When do we start?"

Chapter 16

Several weeks later, MacKenzie frantically tore apart her normally tidy office. She'd spent nearly all of her spare time over the past month working on the illustrations for the new comic book everyone was hoping would save Andrea's shop. Kevin had written a cute, tongue-in-cheek story about a catering shop owner named Annie who moonlighted as a superhero, saving good people all over the world from burnt, poisoned, or simply poorly-prepared food. Annie Saves the World was fun and funny, and MacKenzie thought it had the potential to become very popular as a sort of niche collector's item.

A box of the first issue had already been delivered to the hotel for the auction that started in three hours, where people would be able to read a copy, and then bid on several ways of getting themselves written in as various characters. Kevin had picked up the box from the printers and taken it too the hotel himself, so she hadn't seen the final books, and she hoped they'd turned out well.

But the big illustration boards she'd prepared to show off the style of art she'd used were all missing.

"Kevin? Have you seen my storyboards for Annie? I can't find them anywhere!"

He poked his head out from the front of the shop. "I took them to the hotel with the books. Didn't I tell you?"

She rolled her eyes and let out an exasperated sigh. "No, you did not. And I wanted to check them over one more time before I took them - I thought I told you that."

He shrugged. "Well, they're there now, so too late now. I saw them, and they look fine. You need to stop worrying and go get dressed. It's formal tonight, remember? You can't go like that."

Kenzie looked down at her jeans and Batman t-shirt. "You're right. I should get a Bruce Wayne shirt. Can you see if there are any more in my size on the rack?" She grinned at him, and he shook his head, laughing.

"Go home. We've got this. I'll see you tonight."

He disappeared and she glanced at the mess she'd made, considering a quick straighten before she left.

"Go home, Kenzie!" Kevin called from the other room.

"Fine!" She grabbed her purse and rushed out the door, annoyed at the thought of having to get all dressed up. It couldn't be helped though. This was the night that would seal the fate of Andrea's catering business. The kitchens had been repaired, and she'd gotten a small loan for supplies to prepare the food for tonight from Josh's new company, which was doing better than anyone had thought it would. If they could raise ten thousand dollars tonight, it would be enough to get Taste the World back in the black.

It took a full hour to shower, dress, deal with her hair and apply makeup, but MacKenzie thought she looked pretty good by the time the doorbell rang at six-thirty. Judging by the look in Josh's eyes when she opened the door, he thought so too.

"Ready to do this?" he asked, holding out his arm. She took it and locked the door, walking carefully in the low heels she'd picked out to go with the dress.

"Ready as I'll ever be. Did the set-up go okay at the hotel? I wanted to be there, but Kevin kept finding stuff for me to do at the shop, and he kept disappearing himself..."

Josh laughed as he helped her into the car. "Everything looks great. And I think you're going to be very pleased with how the comic books turned out. Your art is amazing. people are going to love it - and you."

She rolled her eyes. "They don't have to love me, they need to love Annie. She's the star of the show."

"We'll see." Josh smiled, the sort of smile people had when they were hiding something. MacKenzie was suddenly nervous.

"There's something you're not telling me. What are you hiding?"

He shrugged. "It's a surprise."

"I hate surprises." She pretended to pout, her stomach flipping as he pulled into the parking lot. What on earth could they have done?

"Don't worry about it," Josh said, helping her out of the car. "Everything's going to be just fine - you'll see."

She walked in beside him and was immediately swallowed up in a sea of people, most of them wearing jewelry worth more than all of her assets combined. She talked and laughed her way through the crowd, getting separated from Josh at some point as she tried to make her way to the auction tables.

When she finally did, she stopped short, unable to believe what she was seeing. Right there in huge block lettering, the title of the series read "MacKenzie Saves the World", instead of Annie, in deference to Andrea. It had to be a mistake, but there was no way to fix it now, and she had no idea how she was going to explain such a huge faux pas to Andrea.

"Surprise." Josh spoke quietly in her ear, and she turned with a frown.

"What do you mean? This is horrible! Andrea's going to be so--"

"I love it, MacKenzie. It's how it should have been from the start."

MacKenzie turned to see Josh's sister standing on her other side, a wide smile on her face. "You knew?"

Andrea nodded. "We all did. It was Kevin's idea, and Josh and I loved it. We knew you'd never do it if you had a choice, so we sort of did it for you. After all, you are the one saving the world, you know. If it wasn't for you, none of this would be possible."

MacKenzie shook her head, blinking back tears. "It's certainly not just me - we all did this. I...I don't know what to say."

Kevin came up behind Andrea and gave her a quick kiss on the cheek before turning to MacKenzie.

"Say thank you, and then come along to the podium. You're the one everyone will want to see, and it's time to get this auction started."

* * * * *

Josh put the last of the folding chairs on the cart and signaled to the hotel worker he could take them away. The kitchen was nearly clean and he'd sent Andrea home with Kevin an hour ago. The auction had been a huge success, with MacKenzie's new namesake comic bringing in enough money to surpass their goal by nearly eight thousand dollars. He looked over at the auction table where she was just finishing packing up the large pieces of artwork that would be shipped off or picked up by new owners over the next week.

Her hair was falling out of the neat braid it had started in, her shoes were lying near the boxes and she'd hiked her dress up and secured a good chunk of the silvery cloth with a rubber band - something he was pretty sure would give whoever designed the dress a heart attack if they were to see it treated so casually.

She was easily the most beautiful woman he'd seen all night, even in her disheveled state.

"Is this the last of it?" he asked, going to help her. All he wanted now was to get her home and ask her the question he'd been dying to ask for weeks now.

"Yes, thank God." She winced as she slid her feet back into her shoes. "Ready to go?"

"Absolutely." He took the heaviest boxes and led the way to the car, stowing everything in the back. They could drop them off at the store tomorrow. "Can I offer you a beer? Glass of wine, maybe?"

She leaned her head back against the seat as he drove and let out a sigh.

"As long as I can put my feet up, you can take me anywhere you want." Turning her head, she grinned. "And yes, a drink would be nice."

She'd shucked her shoes again by the time they got to his place, and he walked around to her door and swung her up into his arms, thrilled when she laughed at his dramatic gestures.

"I can walk, really. My feet are tough." She didn't struggle though, despite her arguments, and her hands clung to his neck as he struggled with the keys to the front door.

"Your feet have taken enough punishment for the night, I think." He deposited her on his couch, placing her feet on the wide ottoman. "There. Now what can I get you? I have a Merlot and a Rose open, if either of those sound good."

"Merlot, please."

He went and got two glasses of wine, whistling to himself as he poured. Checking his pocket for the millionth time, he went back to the living room, his stomach twisting in either excitement or nervousness. Maybe a little of both.

He shouldn't have been surprised that in the short time he'd been gone, MacKenzie had stretched out full-length on the couch, and was sound asleep.

He thought about moving her to his bed, but decided not to wake her. Instead, he put the wine glasses on an end table and covered her with throw blanket. Sitting back in his favorite chair with another throw, he put his feet up and turned off the light.

* * * * *

The next morning MacKenzie stretched, trying to remember why her muscles were so sore, and how her bed had gotten so soft. Her hands and feet both hit barriers before she opened her eyes and recognized Josh's living room.

And the man himself, fast asleep in his chair across from where she lay on his couch.

She smiled at how peaceful he looked. The past month had been so busy, but they'd made time for each other and she'd gotten to know him - not just what he liked and how he thought, though they'd certainly spent plenty of time talking about...everything, but she knew his expressions, his habits, every line and crease on his face. And everything she knew about him just made him that much more dear to her. She couldn't imagine life without this amazing, resilient man.

Careful to be quiet, she moved the blanket aside and stood, unable to resist just one more stretch up high overhead. When her heels finally touched down and she looked over at Josh, he was looking at her, something in his eyes that she couldn't quite decipher.

"You're beautiful," he said, setting his own blanket aside. She rolled her eyes at him as he rose and came toward her.

"My hair's a mess, this dress is trashed, and I'm sure my makeup's all over my face. But thank you."

He leaned down for a kiss and she met him half-way, surprised when he released her quickly.

"Everything okay?"

He nodded, reaching into his pocket. "Better than okay." He pointed to the ottoman. "Can you sit down for a minute?"

Kenzie sat, her stomach flipping in anticipation. And when he knelt in front of her, she could barely focus for the pounding in her chest. He held out a small black box, still closed on the palm of one hand, and grasped her hand with the other.

"You know I love you, MacKenzie. And I can't imagine my life without you. Will you marry me? Please?"

She couldn't have held back a wide smile if she'd tried.

"Of course I'll marry you. I love you so much." She threw her arms around his neck and kissed him, throwing them both off balance. When they were both laughing on the floor, he rolled to his side and held up the box, a teasing glint in his eye.

"Do you want to see your ring now?" The way he said it, the look on his face made her curious.

"Absolutely." She reached for the box, but he pulled it back out of reach. Laughing, he opened it where she couldn't see it, and then slowly lowered it down to eye level.

Kenzie looked at the dark, almost black titanium band inlaid with two lighter bands top and bottom. A pink oval diamond was set deep in the center, the top flush with the band so it wouldn't get caught on things. She stared for a long moment, not sure whether to laugh or cry as Josh took it out of the box and slid it on the ring finger of her left hand. she wiggled her finger, watching the light flash through the stone.

"I can't believe it," she breathed, unable to take her eyes off it. "You had Charade's ring made. How did you do it?"

Josh reached for her hand, bringing it to his lips for a kiss.

"I had Kevin get me your sketches, and took them to a jeweler I know. One of his designers made it happen. You like it?"

MacKenzie shook her head. "No, I love it. You are amazing." She pulled him down for a kiss, needing him close.

"Superhero amazing?" he murmured against her lips, rubbing his nose against hers. She giggled.

"My own personal superhero, without a doubt."

About the Author

A full-time webmistress by day, Jamie DeBree writes steamy, action-packed romantic suspense late into the night. Her goal is to create the perfect blend of sensual attraction, emotional tension and fast-paced adventure, similar to the television crime dramas she's hopelessly addicted to.

Born in Billings Montana, she resides there with her husband and two over-sized lap dogs. She reads in a wide variety of genres including romance, erotica, action/adventure, thriller, horror and literary fiction.

For information on upcoming books and to sign up for her newsletter, please visit JamieDeBree.com.

Other books by Jamie DeBree

Tempest
Desert Heat
Indelibly Inked
Heart Knocks
The Biker's Wench (Fantasy Ranch 1)
The Minister's Maid (Fantasy Ranch 2)
The Handyman's Harem Girl (Fantasy Ranch 3)
Sleep With Me (Be With Me 1)
Deadly Chai (BeauTEAful Summer)
Jasmine Betrayal (BeauTEAful Summer)
English Breakfast (BeauTEAful Summer)
Indelibly Inked
Flame & Stone (Dunning Manor 1)

9 781732 178984